Also by Alison Baker

Loving Wanda Beaver

How I Came West, and Why I Stayed

Happy Hour

HAPPY HOUR

Stories by

Alison Baker

Tickenoak Publications
Orleans, Mass.
2014

Happy Hour

www.alisonbaker.com

Most of the stories in this collection
were previously published in the following:
"Bodie's Glen" in *ZYZZYVA*; "Thousands Live!" in
The Gettysburg Review; "North of Mount Shasta" and
"One Owner, Runs" in *Story Magazine*; "I'll Meet You
There" in *Minnetonka Review*; "Popeye's Theorem" in
Hospital Drive; "Walk In the Dark" in *Best Fiction;*
"Happy Hour" in *The Atlantic Monthly*

Library of Congress Control Number: 2014938052

ISBN: 978-0692-02-559-8

Tickenoak Publications
Orleans, Mass.

Jacket image: *Jack's Graduation*

For Hans, again

Contents

BODIE'S GLEN

Decay is inherent in all component things!
Work out your salvation with diligence.

– Buddha

Harley Moon had tried Mary Kay, but it
didn't give him enough scope. It was safer than
setting chokers in the woods, and the company
provided terrific resources – training, supplies,
inspiration; but though there were things about the
work that he truly loved, being a cog in a giant
machine was not one of them.

So he had left Mary Kay and gone into the
business for himself. It would be a while before he
was socking away vast amounts in money market
accounts or eco-vacationing in the Galapagos, but
his clientele was slowly expanding, and to his
surprise his income from doing makeovers had now
surpassed his income from selling homegrown.

What Harley loved was the intimacy of
mucking around with the beauty of women. He
found he was terribly moved by the griefs and
hopes of the women whose faces he tenderly coated

with foundation.

"I always thought," more than one woman said, "there would come a time when I'd be comfortable with my body." She'd close her eyes as Harley dipped his finger into a pot of rouge and began to stroke it softly onto her cheekbone. "But here I am, thirty-seven, and my body has begun to disintegrate."

Harley never knew what to say in response. He could protest that every woman was beautiful, but it wasn't true. The first few times he gave a makeover to someone really ugly, or whose breath could choke a toad, he had to grit his teeth. But then he found that he had got caught up in the process: he was fascinated with the challenge, not just of obscuring blemishes and enhancing skin tone, but of seeking out a woman's hidden longings, her inner – as it were – self.

"You mean, like, my inner child might pop to the surface if I wore makeup?" Linda, his ex-wife, said.

Several times a year Harley's suppliers sent him samples of the new shades and textures for the coming season, and he would traipse across the meadow to Linda's cabin to spend an evening trying them out on her. He knew her so well that when he added the last upward sweep of mascara and the final glossy touch to her lips and stood back to look at the finished product, his wrists tingled and tears came to his eyes. He thought it must be the way an artist saw each new rendition of a subject he painted again and again; with every effort it came one step closer to some vision that lurked obsessively inside, waiting for fulfillment.

In fact, over the years he had come to know

many of the women in Bodie's Glen nearly as well. He would drive up a dirt road in the rain to a mobile where a thin line of smoke was rising from the chimney, and as he reached for his samples case and the portable mirror a curtain moved; then the door swung open and the woman of the house stood there, waiting for him to come down the muddy little path.

He knew she waited not for the makeup, not even for Harley Moon himself, but for the possibilities that he carried with him. When she closed her eyes and felt Harley's hands gently rewriting her face, she could believe anything.

"Women like men to touch them, Harley," Linda said, but Harley knew that it was deeper, more important than that: the transformation of a woman's surface changed something inside her. He was humbled by this, and thought that a doctor must feel the same way when he cured someone of cancer, or a priest, when he heard a particularly hard-won confession and pronounced that a sin was forgiven.

"You're a lucky man," Case observed. "To have found your niche, and found it lucrative."

"I wouldn't call it lucrative," Harley said.

"Nevertheless," Case said, "you make more money from one tube of lipstick than I have made from years of poetry."

"Yeah, but you'll outdo me in one swell foop when you sell your first poem to the New Yorker," Harley said. "They pay in the six digits, don't they?"

"I'm not in it for the money," Case said.

Like Harley, Case had moved from job to job over the years, green chaining at the mill, cello-

3

wrapping at The Fruit Concern during the Christmas rush, working with the reforestation crews on the steep, clearcut hills above the Glen. But he was also a poet. He was forever mailing poems to little magazines Harley had never heard of. Before he sealed the envelope he'd let Harley read them, and Harley would be impressed all over again with the way Case could evoke a certain mood, a strong feeling, with the arrangements of words on the page. Case had talent. But he never seemed to get anywhere.

"If one doesn't want to teach," Case would say, pausing to suck smoke from one of his filterless cigarettes, "there is no place in poetry to *go*."

And Harley supposed that Case did not have a bad life, drifting with his bottle of Scotch through Bodie's Glen of an evening, sitting next to someone's stove or out on their steps for a chat and a drink, and then weaving his way back through the wet grass to his own singlewide to write about it.

Last year a marvelous thing had happened. Harley had stopped for a fill-up at Wendell's Food 'n' Gas, and when he went inside to pay, Wendell called, "Just the man we need. Harley here," he said to the young woman standing at the counter, "used to live on the lam. He knows a thousand places to camp hereabouts."

"Used to, but the Feds have the forest sewed up tight these days," Harley said, handing Wendell a twenty. "Five days max in one place."

"That sucks," the woman said. She shifted her backpack and looked him up and down. "You were living outside the law?"

Harley shook his head. "Just living the

low-rent life."

"Exactly what the young lady's looking for," Wendell said, handing Harley his change.

"I've got a couple of acres you could camp on," Harley said, eyeing her backpack. "No plumbing or anything, though."

She looked at him with a little sneer. "I know," she said, "how to dig a latrine."

She dug it that afternoon, but it never got used. By the time she had dug the hole, pitched her tent, and taken a shower in Harley's bathroom, Harley was in love. He invited her to stay for dinner, and at the end of the meal he pushed back his chair and looked across the table at her. She was staring at the candle flame with half-closed eyes, and he thought she was the most beautiful woman he had seen lately.

"So," she said, lifting her eyes to meet his, "you want to make me up, or what?"

"You don't – " he started to say, but he had to clear his throat. "You don't need it. You're so beautiful." His breath was short and his throat was thick as he choked out, "Stay with me tonight."

"Sure," she said.

It was a simple as that. The next morning she took down the tent and piled her gear in his shed.

Daphne was a freelance wilderness guide. She worked, for the most part, in Alaska, but she also covered Montana and British Columbia, and she was well-versed in running the Green, the Colorado, and the Wild and Scenic Rogue rivers. She sometimes helped out some friends who led llama treks in the Cascades, and she did women's groups, Elderhostels, and even private hunting parties. In the winter she pitched a tent in some mild climate and lived off her earnings. If they ran out she waitressed till the wilderness opened up in the spring.

That winter, though, she stayed with Harley. Every day when he came home from selling makeup she would be sitting in the living room with a bottle of beer, the music in her headset cranked up so loud he could hear little voices coming out of her ears. She'd be reading some magazine – *Outside, Field & Stream, Big Game Adventures* – and when she felt the door slam she looked up and smiled and put down her magazine. Afterwards she would take off her headset and come out to the kitchen to watch him make supper.

Harley thought about her all the time. Glancing away from a client's eyes to dip the little applicator into a pot of eye shadow, he would picture Daphne's eyelids, which had a natural blue-black sheen to them, like a bruise, when she first got up in the morning. And listening to other women talk about their wrinkles and spots, he sometimes let his thoughts stray just a bit toward Daphne, who seemed perfectly unconcerned about her looks.

That was what he marveled at: the way she accepted herself. She was on the heavy side; her muscular thighs were pockety with cellulite, and when she was on all fours her stomach tended to flop, but she never seemed to worry about it. She moved through life like a big hefty cat, stalking across the days as if they were laid down for just that purpose. She took what was given to her without a thank you.

Even her snoring excited him, as if, without knowing it, she was revealing some part of

herself in the darkness that she would never have
shown in the light of day. When she inhaled he felt
as if he was on a raft being carried along on a thick,
rough current; and after teetering for long
precarious seconds at the very top of a waterfall, he
plunged down the foaming, bubbling rapids of her
exhalation. As he lay in the dark he could hear, in
the roaring whitewater of her breath, the cascading
notes of the canyon wren and the thin cries of bank
swallows, and he could almost feel the spray in his
face and the hot sun of the Southwest on his
shoulders. Then she choked a little, snorted and
grumbled in her sleep, and turned over on her side;
and Harley reached over to gently unwind the cord
from around her neck and remove the headset from
her ears and place it on the bedside table before he
turned over, too, and fell asleep.

The very nature of the season was different
that year; the heavy grey clouds that draped the
mountains were like a cool, moisturizing mask
lying over the clogged pores of the earth's skin;
when spring came the clouds would lift and flowers
and grass and leaves would burst from the ground
like music. Harley's clients, too, blossomed under
his hands as he powdered and tinted their faces, and
when at last they turned to the mirror they gasped
at their own radiance.

But when warm weather came Daphne
packed up and headed out; she had a women's
group kayaking in the San Juans in May, and some
schoolteachers from New York coming to get a
taste of the Montana wilderness before the snows
even melted from the mountains. In fact she was
scheduled tight all through the summer, up through
the fall, when she would be guiding some lawyers

from Century City to a place in the Canadian
Rockies where they could shoot Dall sheep.

"Daphne," Harley said, taking her face in
his hands and holding it, looking into her eyes,
looking at the little scar where a piece of barbed
wire had once whipped through space to lash her
cheek. He cleared his throat. "Daphne. Say you'll
come back."

"Harley," she'd said, "the kind of life I
live, I could be dead in a flash."

Linda Moon made her living collecting
pollen from wildflowers for a pharmaceutical
company, and it was when she was looking for the
Gentner's fritillary she'd seen in bloom last spring
that she stumbled over a body in the woods. She
did not literally stumble over it, but afterwards that
was the sense she had of it: she was walking
happily down the logging road, gazing into the
gloom of the pre-dawn woods, when she suddenly
saw a gleam of white under the oaks, and her heart
stopped so thoroughly it left her brain without
oxygen for, she was sure, a long ten seconds. She
stood in the road trying to catch her breath and
suddenly the sun rose over the top of Elk
Mountain. She raised her hand to fend it off.

She took a breath, stepped off the road, and
walked through the wet grass to where the woman
lay face down, one arm flung out to the side, a pale
hip curving sensuously out of the leaves. Linda
leaned over and touched the back of the woman's
neck; the skin was wet with dew. Linda knew she
should then slide her hand down the neck and feel
for a pulse, just in case, but she didn't do it. She
stood up and wiped her hand on her jeans.

She knew the woman was dead, and she

was afraid if she turned the body over the face would be gone. She stood there as robins called and the mules a mile away in the Butlers' barnyard brayed as Mr. Butler brought out their breakfast, and a thousand difficult thoughts tumbled around in her brain. She loved Harley, even after all these stupid years she loved him. Since their divorce they had drifted down different roads in different directions but she had thought that had led her to know him even better than when they lived together. And she had been pleased, really, when he got his new little girlfriend.

"You must be Daphne," she had said. "I've heard so much about you." Daphne was fat but she was blonde and if you looked very closely, or very carelessly, at her, you might imagine you could see something in her face that Harley also had in his.

"And you're – ?" Daphne said.

"Linda," Linda said. "Linda Moon."

"Oh yeah," Daphne said. "The ex."

Linda did not look again at the dead woman. She went home by way of the shortcut along the creek that bordered her property and Harley's, and went into her own cabin without looking across the field toward his. There she sat down on the sofa and stared at the wall.

Then she said aloud, "What am I doing!" These were the first words she had spoken since she found the body, and the sound of her voice startled her. She was able then to look up the telephone number of the county sheriff, and she gave him a call.

"Oh, Linda," Case said, seizing her hand. "I should have been with you."

"Case," she said, wresting her hand back,

"it was just another body in the woods."

And so it was. Not only were the woods full of the dead – moles dropped in the road by owls, piles of insects who had expired after one last mating frenzy, and, in hunting season, the viscera of deer strewn along the side of the road – but Linda had found a human body before. It had been long ago, in another place, but the time of day was the same: she'd been out before dawn, probably stumbling home from an all-night party, and in a lush glade on the edge of the campus she had nearly stepped on a man lying on his back in the leaves. Thinking he was asleep, she had leaned over to peer into his face to see if she knew him and had found herself gazing into sightless wide-open eyes.

Afterwards she had gone to the college counselor for a few weeks and sobbed about death, and about her mother, and about how stupid she felt in most of her classes, and toward the end of the semester she and Harley had dropped out, bought the white bus and named it Nirvana, and headed for Alaska.

Now Nirvana, covered with lichens and pine needles, stood in the tall grass behind Harley's cabin, and Linda couldn't get the dead woman out of her mind. It was as if a snapshot of the clearing were tacked up in the front corner of her brain, and it caught her mind's eye every time she tried to think. When she turned to look directly at it, her other thoughts were at once stilled, much the way the woods had gone abruptly silent when she first glimpsed the white curve of the woman's hip.

She was not beset by a fear of death, or even of violence, but she couldn't help seeing that everything around her was destined to become compost. This was easy to see in fallen trees and the dying weeds of late summer, of course, but she also saw it in the paint peeling off the windowsills of her cabin and the frayed sleeves of old shirts, and when she heard on NPR that yellow-shafted flickers had been drilling holes in the space shuttle she knew it was another indication of the temporary nature of everything.

"You're aware of your own mortality now," Case said. "I've seen it many times. We hit forty and we realize we've failed. If you haven't made it by now, you're out of luck."

"Made what?" she said.

"In my case, the great American epic poem," he said. "In yours, the discovery of some lost popcorn flower. Our efforts will come to nothing in the end." He leaned over and touched her cheek. "Mark my words."

Despite his much-vaunted sensitivity, Linda thought, Case knew nothing. He had never been able to interpret life accurately, starting with that first morning he'd wandered into Bodie's Glen. She had been taking a shower under the ten-gallon drum Harley had winched up into a fir tree behind Nirvana when Case stepped out of the woods. In those days Linda had thought that love and good will could be the salvation of the world, so she had stifled her scream at the sudden appearance of a stranger and simply waved. "Good morning," she called. "Sleep well?"

At the sight of a beckoning naked woman Case had stood stock-still. "My god, you're magnificent," he said, and she felt as if she should kick up her heels and whinny.

Apparently he had been struck to the depths of his very soul by her beauty, because even after he met Harley he had continued to follow Linda around the glen, dedicating poems to her and sometimes seizing her hand and pressing it fervidly to his lips. She had been delighted and amused for a while, and then annoyed; but in time it had come to seem natural, just Case's Way. When she and Harley got divorced Case had spent an agitated year or two, so hopeful and spaniel-like she had almost felt sorry for him, but when he finally understood that Linda's new state of non-matrimony indicated no change in his own condition, his agitation had subsided, and he had sunk into a permanent mode of hopeless devotion.

Case picked up his bottle. "Shall I stay tonight, Linda?"

"No," she said. It was their little ritual. She kissed his cheek and watched him walk away in the dark. Someone who claimed to love her so intensely, whose life had been focused on her for so many years, ought to have known that it wasn't just the finding of another body in the woods that had shaken her so, she thought.

Of course, she hadn't told him that she'd thought the body was Daphne's. Or that her immediate response was that if Daphne lay dead among the fritillaries it was because Harley had left her there.

But the body was not Daphne's, which Linda would have known if she had dared to peer into the face, which was not eaten away at all, nor even dark with pooled blood, since the woman had not been dead very long.

"I don't like to alarm people unnecessarily," a red-haired detective had said when he came to take her statement, "but you were

lucky, ma'am, that you weren't any earlier up
there, or the perp wasn't any later."

"The perp?" she said. "You don't think it
was domestic violence?"

The red-haired detective stared at her
without blinking. "Ma'am," he said, "those stats
on domestic violence have been recently debunked.
The fact is that most crime victims are attacked by
strangers." He shifted his stance, but still didn't
blink. "Besides which, ma'am, when you come
upon someone disposing of evidence, they're likely
to be surprised and alarmed. I would not vouch for
your safety at the instant of discovery."

She felt sick with relief that she hadn't
voiced her suspicions to the police. She shivered to
think of happy-go-lucky Harley, a sort of golden
retriever of a man, in the hands of this emotionless
detective. Harley would crack a couple of jokes;
then, when the red-haired detective continued to
ask in a flat tone, "Where were you at three
o'clock on the morning of the fifth? Where did
you say this woman Daphne has gone?" the rims
of Harley's blue eyes would redden, and his nose
would begin to glow, and before long he would
probably start to cry. That had always been his
reaction to accusation, whether he was guilty or
not.

She was having her morning coffee, a
couple of weeks after she'd found the body, when a
white Bronco drove up into the yard and the red-
haired detective himself got out. She went outside
and watched him cross the yard.

"Ms. Moon? Jesse Winchester," he said,
not offering his hand. "There's some things I'd
like to go over with you in case we missed
something." He squinted over at Harley's cabin.

"You any relation to Harley Moon?"

"My ex-husband," Linda said. "Why?"

"Funny sort of thing, living next door to your ex," Jesse Winchester said.

"We split our land," Linda said. "We're friends."

"So how long you been divorced?" he said.

"Seven years," Linda said. "Why?"

"I'm going to level with you, Ms. Moon." He stared at his feet, which were encased in green leather cowboy boots. His hands, hanging by the thumbs from his belt, were deeply freckled, and his pale fingers were long. "I want to ask you out to dinner."

"What?" she said.

"I couldn't just call you up out of the blue," he said. "I needed some pretext."

"So you come up and make me think you're going to arrest me or something?" she said. "That's a great beginning."

"You think it's a beginning?" he said, looking up hopefully.

"I think I'm a little pissed off."

"Oh," he said glumly. He looked off at the hills behind her cabin.

They stood in silence for a moment and then Linda said, "So are you asking or what?"

Jesse Winchester folded his arms over his chest. "You make me feel like an adolescent," he said. "I feel like a dope."

"Don't blame me for that," she said. "Are you spying on me?"

Jesse Winchester's face went very still, and he said, "The department doesn't spy, I don't spy."

"I don't think I trust you."

"Well, who *do* you trust?" He looked around the yard. "I used to work in New York, but it got to be too much for me. Murder here, murder there. Drugs and more drugs."

"But you're in the same line of work here."

"I love it," he said. "It's always a different puzzle, a different set of clues. I meet a lot of people. I get to go a lot of places I wouldn't otherwise." He looked at her and looked quickly away. "I would never have come up here without you found that body. You know what a bad rep this place has? 'Keep out of Bodie's Glen,' they said when I started. 'Take backup with you.'"

"That's old news," she said. "That was Jack Jensen and those guys. They're long gone. Things are cleaned up."

"Still a lot of drugs, though," Jesse said. "I myself, personally, am not interested in potheads. It's not worth any law enforcement agent's time, I'll tell you that. There's bigger fish to fry."

"Well," she said, "it is immaterial to me."

He took to coming around in the mornings, and she would take him with her into the woods and up on the dry hills to collect pollen. Afterwards they sat outside drinking coffee in the shade. Jesse suffered from the sun; the whites of his eyes took on a fluorescent effect in his fiery face, and droplets of perspiration appeared spontaneously on his skin. Linda had never much cared for redheads.

In fact Jesse Winchester was not the sort of person that Linda would normally be interested in at all. He was an inch shorter than she was and he had not read a book since high school. He had a funny attitude she could not quite put her finger on: he knew things and he didn't know them. He had experience with all kinds of people, and when he spoke of them he spoke, for the most part, with respect, as if he understood why they were the way they were, and what life had handed them. He wasn't a bigot. Yet he expected the worst from people who lived in Bodie's Glen.

"But *I* live here," Linda said.

"The exception that proves the rule, Ms. Moon," Jesse Winchester said.

She found herself pushing what she thought might be the envelope containing Jesse's tolerance – telling him things about her past that she expected him to recoil from, and expounding on her liberal views about politics, sex, drugs, and anything else she could think of. Jesse Winchester sat listening with interest, his head cocked, his pale eyes on something below him – his feet, the ground. Nothing shocked him. He wore doubleknit trousers and polo shirts, and around his neck he wore a gold chain.

One day she asked how the case was going.

"We're working on it," he said. "We're following up some leads."

She sighed. "I wish you would tell me about it. I feel as if it's my case."

Jesse Winchester sat back and scratched his ear. "You shouldn't get so involved," he said. "It's wrong to get so involved in things like this unless you're being paid. I could tell you stories about people who follow the cops around, looking for bloodstains and such. Calling up with clues all the time. Know what we call them? Ghouls. These are people you wouldn't want to be one of."

"But I found the body," Linda said. "Don't you think it's normal to want to know how she got there?"

"Just take my word for it," Jesse said.

"Leave it alone."

She frowned in annoyance. "Why do you come here, anyway?" she said.

For once Jesse looked right at her, his mouth open a little. "I'll be honest with you, Ms. Moon," he said. "I want to sleep with you."

Linda stared at him until his red face brightened alarmingly, and he closed his mouth and looked away.

"I'm sorry," he said. "I'm out of line."

"I don't think we're right for each other," she said. "I think we come from opposite ends of the spectrum. I think our values are very different and I think we could never make a go of it in the long run."

He nodded gloomily.

"So this is sex and sex only, Jesse," she said. She touched his elbow, which was the only part of him she could reach without having to make some kind of production out of it. He turned toward her so eagerly she thought her heart would crack with the sudden hot tenderness that flowed into it.

"I brought a condom," he said.

Harley was aghast. He set down his samples case and took off his fedora. "Linda, Jesse Winchester is a *narc*. He was behind all that harassment Jack Jensen used to get."

"Oh, I don't think so," she said.

"Linda, Linda, Linda," Harley said. "What has middle age done to you?"

"What's that supposed to mean, Harley?" she said, feeling suddenly puffy around the hips.

"Where are your principles?" he said. "Where is your loyalty?"

"To what?"

He put his fedora back on so he could take her upper arms in his hands and pull her close to him. "Honey, to our *generation*," he said. "To our times. To what our whole life has stood for."

"Harley," she said, "I didn't criticize your girl guide. Don't criticize my cop."

Harley spent that summer moping his way through the days, making half-hearted cold calls on potential clients, staring listlessly at the cosmetics catalogues that flowed in gleaming with the new fall shades. He felt out of control. He felt as if in that first half hour at Wendell's Food 'n' Gas he had handed Daphne the keys to his heart, and she had jammed them into her back pocket and left without returning them. Now he could picture her bounding through the wilderness, leaping as nimbly as a goat from rock to rock across roaring rivers, balancing on mossy logs over deep chasms; and every time her left buttock moved, the keys to his heart inched a little higher in her pocket, till they were dangling over the edge, kept in by one link in a worn-out key chain that was snagged on a fraying thread.

When he stepped outside for his morning pee he would look across the meadow toward Linda's cabin, and more often than not he saw Jesse Winchester's Bronco parked behind her truck. Seeing it there, glistening with dew, made him think of all the sad parties he'd been to in his youth, all the excitement that had flowed in the nights and ebbed with the dawns.

His entire youth had been spent with Linda, all the youth that counted, anyway. He'd loved her from the first week of college, when he'd been working the dorms selling peyote and walked into her room to see her sitting on her bed in her little pink nightie.

"What's it like?" she'd said, and he wouldn't sell her any. There were some people who were not cut out to hallucinate and Linda was one of them. She drifted along about three feet from reality as a matter of course; drugs would have severed the tie completely. She was a woman who needed a great deal of protection.

When she broke down after finding the dead guy he'd taken her off to Alaska, where the air was clean and her low grades were irrelevant, and so were his. They lived in Nirvana in the shadow of Mount McKinley, and he thought they'd been happy. He could still feel the way the cold morning air in Alaska would slice right into his nose, and smell the fecund smell of the taiga, full of the odors of pure snow and heavily-furred mammals.

That's probably where Daphne was right now, her little tan tent pitched in the very spot where he and Linda had parked Nirvana, where they had cooked endless pots of rice and wrapped themselves in mosquito netting night after night. Daphne was really living that life, while he had just played at it, and then given up and come back down to Bodie's Glen to work for Jack Jensen and build a house and become a middle-aged man. A man that a woman like Daphne might come to in the fall, but would leave when summer rolled around. A man heading into the winter of his life.

"Go after her, man," Case said. "Follow your dream."

"I don't even know her schedule," Harley said.

"The course of true love never did run

true," Case said. "God, Harley, do you know the pain I feel when I think of Linda with that detective?"

"Linda's just feeling her age," Harley said. "She needs reassurance."

Case put his hands over his face. "She could have come to me."

"Well, for that matter, she could have come to *me* if she was that desperate," Harley said. "I would have obliged for old times' sake."

"I never really minded when she was with you," Case said through his fingers. "It seemed right, somehow. Because both of you are my friends. But this other person."

"But you have the consolation of poetry," Harley said.

Case lowered his hands and stared at him. "My muse has gone silent, Harley."

At least Case knew where Linda was, Harley thought irritably. He could wait and watch and be ready in case Linda needed him; he could hover outside the goddamned bedroom door if he really wanted to.

But Daphne was out where Harley had never been and would never go. She was in constant danger from wild animals, steep precipices, lightning strikes and, for that matter, rich lawyers with guns. Even now she could be lying dead in some wilderness.

Maybe Case was right. Maybe he should go after her. He imagined himself in his baggy jeans and his Rolling Thunder Review tee shirt, traipsing through the duff with his makeup case in his hand, panting to keep up with the Wall Street brokers in skin-tight black shorts and fluorescent tank tops who raced after her through the woods.

He sighed, and the feeling of gloom that had shuffled along in his footsteps all summer inched closer, sliding its gray arms around his waist and laying its sad head on his back. He could feel gloom's nose between his shoulder blades, pressing into his spine.

As autumn came on and the sun's heat thinned, clouds gathered behind the mountains to peer over into the valley and wave forks of lightning in a distant promise that the rains were on the way. The dogwoods had eased through their second blooming of the year and stood pale on the sides of the ravines, and the vine maples were brightening into the brilliant red that would last until the first rain hit.

Harley felt as if all of Bodie's Glen was holding its collective breath, waiting to see if Daphne would return. The cooling air gave him a strange feeling of urgency, and he rushed from one client to another, eager to ease their pain and lead them out of their unhappy darkness into the light of beauty. He smiled as he bent toward woman after woman, applying a beige liquid foundation to one, a peachish powder to another, reshaping eyebrows, defining lips; he could feel their faces changing shape and texture under his hands. The air was full of smoke from dying wildfires in the hills. The days were growing shorter.

It was Wendell who told Harley that Linda's body had been identified. "Already dead when she got here's what I heard," Wendell said. "This gal's husband carted her up from Sacramento and dumped her in the woods."

"Sacramento?" Harley said.

"In the back of a pickup, under a tarp,"

Wendell said. "Drove up the interstate till he crossed the state line. Then up through the Glen till the road ended." He folded his arms and glared down an aisle at some snickering boys.

"Why here, do you suppose?" Harley said.

Wendell shrugged. "Probably been here before. Hunting season, maybe."

Harley nodded and said, "I'll ask Linda. Maybe the narc has the details."

Wendell shook his head. "I got to tell you, Harley, I'm a little surprised that's kept on this long. Animal lust I can understand, but what do they talk about?"

"Hell if I know, Wendell," Harley said.

"Well, judge not that ye be not judged." Wendell raised his voice. "You fellas just here to enjoy yourselves, or you planning to buy some of that tissue?" He looked back at Harley. "Anything from your little gal yet?"

"No," Harley said sadly. He reached for a package of Hostess Sno-Balls.

"I'll let you know if I hear anything," Wendell said, ringing them up. "One way *or* the other, Harley. Ah, Charmin," he said to the boys, who had appeared behind Harley at the counter. "Now that'll feel good when you're out in the woods."

Out in the parking lot, Harley got into the cab of his truck and unwrapped the Sno-Balls. He closed his eyes and tried to imagine himself heaving Linda's naked body into the back of the truck in the dark, then taking the tarp from the woodpile and tucking it around her. He licked a shred of coconut off his lip and imagined starting the engine, pulling out onto the road, and heading for Alaska.

The imaginary Harley in his imaginary truck tooled on up the old Al-Can highway, a cloud of dust rising behind him, the rumble and rattle of gravel deafening. The dead Linda under the tarp stayed clean and pristine while Harley's hair and beard grew as thick with road dust as if he'd dropped a keg of pancake makeup on his head. He would drive until he reached the old clearing – in his memory it was green and lush, a crystalline stream babbling gently under the willows, a bald eagle preening in the top of a pine. There he would light a little campfire, smoke a little of the pleasant dope they'd grown that summer, sing a little Cat Stevens.

As darkness fell he would rise from his seat beside the fire, pull the tarp off Linda's body and take her in his arms. He would carry her gently into that good night, up the little ravine where they'd seen the moose, and place her on a bed of dry soft leaves, her body gleaming white in the light of the rising crescent moon.

"Goodnight," he whispered, and he opened his eyes to see the boys from the store leaning against the Chevy pickup beside him, watching him curiously. He started the engine and drove on home.

"Human nature," Jesse told Linda over dinner. "Men are always offing their wives."

Linda leaned her chin on her hand. "I wonder why human beings are so violent."

"Overcrowding," he said. "Familiarity breeds crime."

She watched him eat a cucumber slice. "Is that why you never got married?"

He stopped, fork in mid-air, and looked at

her water glass. "I never said that," he said.

"You mean you were married?"

He didn't move. Finally, still staring at her water glass, he said, "Am."

"What?" Linda said. She leaned toward him. "You *are* married? Right now?"

He met her eyes, a bright flush rising through his cheeks. "Twenty-three years."

"Then," she said, "what are you doing here?"

He put his fork down and looked at his plate, then at the corners of his placemat, then at her water glass again. "My wife and I don't get along," he said to the glass.

"Ah," Linda said. She sat back and carefully aligned the edge of her own placemat with the edge of the table. "Well, why don't you off her then?"

Jesse looked once more at his plate. "Don't think I haven't thought of it," he said. "I'm no different from any other man."

"Every man thinks of killing his wife?"

Jesse Winchester nodded. "In my experience, yes."

Linda gazed out the window for a while. Then she said, "You know, when I first found the body I thought it might be Harley's little girlfriend."

"Daphne? No way," Jesse said.

"You know Daphne?" Linda said in surprise.

He looked at the refrigerator. "She's done some work for the department," he said.

"Work?" Linda said. "Like search and rescue or something?"

"Odd jobs," Jesse said flatly.

"Odd jobs for the sheriff's department," she said. She stared at him for a while. "And you thought Harley killed her."

Jesse pushed his chair back from the table and folded his arms. "In a homicide case everyone with a connection to the victim is a suspect."

"That's why you started coming around, isn't it?" she said. "To check him out."

Jesse frowned. "Maybe at first," he said. "Maybe the first time. Maybe the first time I knocked on your door, I had that in mind. But not the second."

"Does your wife know about me?"

Jesse looked at the floor.

"Let me guess," Linda said. "She thinks you're working nights. Like you're on a stakeout or something."

Jesse shrugged.

"Oh, Jesse," she said. "Why do you stay married?"

He looked up at her. "Why not? You don't love me."

"If I did, would you leave her?" she said.

"In a flat thirty seconds," Jesse said, his unblinking eyes fixed on hers.

For one split second bright planets spun past her ears, rare and endangered flowers were safe, and she and Jesse danced toward each other across a golden meadow, smiling and laughing, reaching for each other's hands. Then she came back to herself.

"It would never work, Jesse," she said.

He looked down at his hands. The cartilage in his ears glowed, and his eyeballs protruded, colorless and glistening, below the sandy eyelashes that stuck out of his translucent eyelids. His hands clutched the edge of the table, his knuckles a bright white among the straight red hairs.

"It might," he said.

She lay awake for a long time that night. Beside her Jesse was awake, too, breathing heavily through his nose, but she did not want to talk to him. Her life had been a waste of time. She had accomplished nothing, and no one had loved her enough. The years had whipped by far too fast, stripping away possibilities as they went, and now there were many things she would never do. She would never have children, she would never be the First Lady, she would never hitchhike through Nigeria. Now, instead of possibilities, the rest of her life seemed full of consolation prizes for people with prodromal senility, like being named Volunteer Envelope Stuffer of the Month. A woman who began something new at midlife would not achieve much.

A woman who took a new lover at midlife couldn't expect much, either. How could she, Linda Fick Moon, have turned into a middle-aged woman who would sleep with a married middle-aged narc?

Sometime after midnight a breeze came through the window and touched her face, and Jesse's hand slid across the sheet into hers. For a long time it lay motionless in her palm, as if it were hoping against hope that her fingers would curl up around it in a sign that things would be all right.

Like Harley, Case felt that all of Bodie's Glen was holding its breath, waiting for something to happen. He closed his eyes and the air throbbed; he felt sick, almost dizzy, as if everything in the Glen, the greens of the vegetation, the gold of the light, the thick gray fog that was the air, all whirled around him as he sat at the center of the vortex with glazed eyes and yellow face, looking like Van Gogh's self-portrait.

"Art is what happens when the blood flows free," he had said aloud one August night as he walked home from Linda's cabin. He had loved the sound of it, he had *exulted* at the sound of it, and he had thrown back his head and raised his hands toward the heavens, where he thought the Pleiades were hurling themselves through the galaxies, and walked that way until his arms were tired and shaking and his hands tingled from lack of blood. He wrote it down on a three-by-five card when he got home.

But the next day he could do nothing with "Art is what happens when the blood flows free;" the day after that it seemed distant and stale; and on the third day he began to feel fear. Lately he couldn't think; it was as if some kind of blood-brain barrier had been raised at the spot where his spine met his skull, and ideas, information, and language could no longer pass from his body into his brain.

Case had always known that after the age of forty the artist's creativity diminished rapidly. He had been lucky to stay afloat this long; luck, or his isolation in Bodie's Glen, or some particularly fortunate arrangement of brain synapses, had enabled him to do good, original work much longer than the average artist. But this obstruction had arisen. He had expected it, he had not dared hope for more reprieve, but still, as he sat in his darkened living room, he felt deprived, abused, as if the music of the spheres had somehow led him on to believe that he was – a special Case.

"Ha," he said aloud. It was a bitter sound,

and he made it again: *Ha. Ha. Ha.*

He pulled the little chain of the banker's lamp he'd bought at Ernst Home Center and a homely circle of light clicked onto his desk. He stared at his arms. They were freckled arms covered with yellow hair; he bent lower and saw – he'd seen it before, but he'd forgotten – they were no longer freckled, they were darkened with liver spots, the melanin-ridden arms of an aging man closing in on a date with skin cancer. He was doomed to lose, bit by bit, the integrity of his integument. And his artistic integrity was necrotizing right along with it.

"Oh, Linda," he moaned, raising his old hands to cover his old face.

He sat that way at his desk for a long time. Then he began pulling out his files of poems. He read them for three hours. They were, really, quite good. The very shape of them on the page brought back to him the time of day he'd written them, the slant of light across a road, the look of Linda's eyes when she was stoned or in those years when she was leaving Harley. He'd caught it, he'd caught his entire life in poetry.

He looked up from the page and saw that no sunlight lay against the curtained window; the sun had sunk below the hills and the Glen lay in the long dusk that led to autumn and the winter rains.

Harley just had to predicate his actions on the supposition that Daphne would return. He had straightened up the shed so that her gear could be stored more efficiently; he'd cleaned out the lairs of the harvestmen from the corners of the house and thrown out the little pyramids of roaches that had accumulated in the ashtrays. Now he was ready to tackle the roof, which by the end of last spring had been leaking steadily in the southeast corner. You couldn't expect a woman to come in out of the rain in order to live under a leak.

He climbed the ladder and walked up to stand on the peak beside the chimney. Below him Nirvana's roof was covered with pine needles and bird poop; across the meadow, Linda's truck was parked in front of her house, and behind it was Jesse Winchester's Bronco. Harley gave it the finger.

On the hill beyond her house was the great herd of crows that had spent the summer there in the woods, screaming and carrying on. Now, as he watched, they began jumping from tree to tree, and then they began to take off, cawing and shrieking. Wave after wave of them headed his way, forty or fifty or more flapping over Linda's house and across the field. The sight of Harley on his roof seemed to catch them by surprise, and as each wave of crows reached his house it rose up and soared high above him, screeching and accusing. As they passed overhead he stood there in great delight with his head thrown back, gazing straight up at the feet clutched up against their bellies, an occasional head cocked sideways and a crowly eye staring back at him.

A door slammed, and Harley looked over at Linda's house to see Jesse Winchester going down the steps. He did not want Jesse Winchester to see him, and he started to duck behind the chimney. But the blood that was stopped up by the crook in his neck as he watched the crows must have spurted into his brain when he looked down, for suddenly everything went black. He stumbled, and slipped, and when he grabbed for the chimney to steady himself his foot caught on a loose shingle and he fell face down with a thud that knocked the wind out of him. He slid gasping for breath toward the eaves, head-first, clutching at shingles, and sailed off the edge of the roof.

Such terrific pain tore through his leg that he thought it must have been wrenched right out of its socket. His boot must have caught in the rain gutter, and now he swung by one foot, his leg connected to the rest of his body by only the skin of his thigh, which was stretched out as thin as an old balloon.

In his younger days a fall from the roof would have been nothing, nothing! He would have landed on his toes and sprung up laughing; or, caught like this by the boot, he would simply have swung himself up, seized the edge of the roof, and calmly lifted his toe out of its trap. Then he would have pushed off from the roof and soared out into the sky in a graceful arc. Such was his light and ethereal body in bygone years that he might have continued to rise, startling the Steller's jays in the top of one of the taller pines and gliding on up to join the crowd of raucous crows. From among their dark bodies he could look down on the earth and see the curve of the planet against the heavens.

A wave of nausea swept over him, and he reached out for the side of the house to stop his body from swinging. A cold hand seized his, and another hand slid across his forehead. He opened his mouth, but no sound came out; he could not breathe.

"Don't try to move," Linda said.

He opened his eyes. He lay flat on the ground, and Linda was leaning over him. "My leg," he whispered.

"I think it's broken, Harley," she said. "Lie still. Jesse's calling an ambulance."

He clutched her hand. "Don't let him into Nirvana."

"Don't worry," she said. "He's not interested in that sort of thing."

"Once a narc, always a narc," Harley said.

And sure enough, at that instant they heard the old familiar creak as the door to Nirvana opened, and Jesse Winchester said, "Jesus fucking Christ."

The world is full of miracles, and right there on that October Saturday there was a bunch of them in Bodie's Glen. It was a miracle that Harley didn't break his neck, and it was a miracle that Linda, following Jesse Winchester out the door, looked across the field just in time to see Harley plunge off the roof of his own house.

Nirvana itself had long been a kind of miracle, a beat-up old formerly white school bus, its windows boarded over, its last trip years in the past; but, inside, full-spectrum fluorescent lights, drip irrigation, recirculating air: a lush garden, a bright hot jungle, a moist, tropical Eden.

"Crunchy on the outside, hot and runny on the inside," was what Daphne had said when she first stepped through the magic door.

And on this miraculous weekend the official paperwork was slow to arrive, so that by Monday, when warrants were issued and officers from the local and county and state levels drove up into Harley's yard and got out of their cars and followed Jesse Winchester up the steps to Nirvana, Nirvana was empty. It was stripped bare – not a lamp, not a piece of rubber tubing, not the blade of a fan, not a leaf of any kind of vegetation. It smelled strongly of chlorine, and it was a little bit damp, as if someone had recently scrubbed it up and hosed it down, but there was no sign it had ever been anything but a beat-up old bus.

Harley drifted in and out of consciousness for some time, falling from a great height toward rich dark earth only to wake up at the instant of impact to find himself whirling around and around in his hospital bed. Or he hurried endlessly through the forest after Daphne, who was just out of sight ahead of him. He tried to run but he could only pull himself along by the branches of trees, dragging his broken leg, which grew longer and longer and pooled and curled along the ground behind him like the train of a wedding gown. He called, "Daphne! Daphne!" to no avail; he could hear the tiny voices leaking out of her headset, and he knew she had it turned up so loud she would never hear him. At times like this he would weep with frustration, and then he might hear someone beside him, fiddling with the tubing that ran into his arm, and the sound of Daphne's little voices would fade, and he would sink gratefully into a drugged sleep.

At other times he was awake and his leg hurt like hell. It had suffered a spiral fracture, as if Harley had twirled to earth like a maple seed and then tried to twirl himself right into the ground. It was one of the worst fractures the orthopods at the regional hospital had ever seen, and they clustered around his x-rays with great pleasure.

"You could have been killed," Case said, waving his hand dramatically. "You could be dead at this very minute."

"Maybe I am," Harley said. "Maybe this is

heaven, and I have you guys to wait on me for eternity." He grinned. "I sure would like to have seen the narc's face."

"Do me a favor," Linda said. "Don't call him that." She sat back in her chair and looked at the television, where football players were silently piling on top of each other. "You know, I think he loved me as much as he could love anyone."

"If that's the best he could do, it doesn't count," Case said.

Linda stuck out her tongue at him. After a minute she said, "Harley, did you ever think of killing me?"

He frowned at her. "Sure."

"You did?" she said in surprise.

"Well, just in passing," he said. "It's not like I planned it out or anything."

She stood up and walked over to the window. "I don't think I ever even imagined killing you. I don't think such an idea would cross my mind. When?" She looked around at him. "When did you think of killing me?"

The rims of his eyes reddened. "Hell, Linda, I don't know. I'm just thinking of times we had fights. You know. You get mad and you say to yourself, 'I could *kill* her.' You never really mean it."

He closed his eyes. In the last few days he had begun to develop a feeling of great longing, a desire to be not just out of bed but to be on the road again, sitting high up in the driver's seat and tooling along through unblemished nature, out into some place where nothing needed fixing. He longed for perfection, he longed for paradise. The faces of his clients drifted past like a long stream of masks, each one perfectly made up.

"I've got it all planned," he said, opening
his eyes again. "We can set Nirvana up as a mobile
beauty lab. Mirrors, lights, soft music. We can
drive right up to people's doors."

Case pulled a cigarette out of his shirt
pocket and tapped it against his knee. "What do
you mean 'we,' white man?"

"Well, Case, I'm going to need someone to
drive," Harley said. "At least till Daphne comes
back."

Case raised his eyebrows and looked at
Linda.

Linda looked out the window again.
"Speaking of Daphne," she said.

Harley could just see the edge of Linda's
face from where he lay, and he watched her jaw
tighten as the color slid up the curve of her cheek.
He closed his eyes again in a hurry. "You never did
like her," he said. "You didn't like her from the
start."

Linda turned around. Harley's unwashed
hair lay flat against his skull, and she saw that his
hairline had slid right up to the crown of his head.
Except for the red eyelids, his face was almost as
white as the thin cotton blankets that covered him.
He looked like an old man.

She did not love Harley any more. She felt
helpless with the knowledge, as if it had swept
through her body like the influenza epidemic of
1918 and left her empty and lifeless. For the first
time in a long time she remembered how happy the
sound of his ankles used to make her when he
walked; she would hear them snapping in the hall
and open the door of her dorm room to see him
bouncing toward her on the balls of his feet, his
mouth half open in what people who didn't like

him called an imbecilic grin. Now the bounce and the cracking were gone, and though the idiot grin was still there, there was less to compensate for it; as time went on it would be harder and harder for people to see that Harley was more than the sum of his imperfect parts.

"Don't be silly," she said. "I hardly knew the child."

Case lit his cigarette and leaned his chair back against the wall. He could feel a poem forming somewhere deep, probably near his omentum, where the best poems originate. It would rise like a mushroom from that fertile region where all that one sees and feels and hears mixes with the bacteria and hope and bile that are the heart of all poetry, there at the edge of that opening that is also a closure, the place of the final choice between rising again into poetry and making a last ignominious exit from the body.

Without him, what would happen to Harley? Or to Linda? As for Daphne, he knew she would come back; even stoolies fall in love. Then Case would take the wheel of Nirvana, and with Linda at his side and Harley strapped in behind them, Daphne in her little headphones holding his hand, they would drive from house to house, and the middle-aged women of Bodie's Glen would lean eagerly toward them, to be touched, to be changed, to be saved.

THOUSANDS LIVE!

Bert listened with growing despair to the frantic reports on the famine. Thousands of people were dying and Bert was doing nothing about it. In his youth that had been a valid topic for debate: should one feel guilty for doing nothing about something that one can do nothing about? But that was before the helplessness of maturity had set in; that was before Bert and his friends had discovered that no matter how vast their intelligence, how good their grades, how physically attractive they were, they lacked the power to effect any change in human nature.

He walked toward the clinic carrying a paper cup of sweet coffee. Damp air fragrant with sea life lay lightly on the sidewalks and drifted in invisible clouds down the alleys, calming the hearts of the psychotic. Gulls sobbed outside fourth-floor windows. Bert drank his coffee through a hole in the plastic lid and handed a woman with one eye a dollar bill. As one of the lucky ones, shouldn't he be doing something?

"Sorry I'm late, Wedge," he said to the gaunt man waiting in the examining room.

"No problem," Wedge said. "I've got all

the time in the world."

"How's Vinnie?" Bert said, sitting down beside him.

"Not good," Wedge said. "His mom's here."

"Ah," Bert said. He gently squeezed Wedge's knee, and then proceeded to measure the pressure of his blood and peer into his orifices. "You're as well as can be expected," he finally said.

"Under the circumstances." Wedge smiled. It was a little joke they had. "What about you, though, Bert? You're not going to have me to kick around forever."

"Don't think I don't worry about it, Wedge," Bert said.

"Maybe you should get into another line of work," Wedge said, buttoning his shirt. "Maybe it's time to get out of death and dying and into something fun."

"The problem with that," Bert said, "is that I think this stuff *is* fun."

"Well, you're one of the lucky ones," Wedge said. "Plenty more where I came from."

"Yeah," Bert said. "I picked the right field for me."

And he had picked the right field. Working with slowly dying people beat the pants off working with, say, trauma victims, who spent most of the doctor-patient relationship in pain and terror. Not that people with terminal illnesses were unafraid; but they had brief respites, moments at night or in the early morning when they could relax a little and philosophize while they played a hand of hearts. A long, slow, dying, as long as the pain was sufficiently alleviated with chemicals, was heartbreaking, and devastating to families, but Bert thought it was preferable to a sudden departure that left everything unfinished.

He had made the mistake of saying this to his mother about halfway through his father's illness. His mother had looked at him with no expression on her face and said, "You don't know beans, Bert."

And Bert supposed he didn't.

After work Bert went out for pizza with some of the nurses, but he found his thoughts drifting away from the people who sat at the long table around him. On the radio this morning he had heard a small boy wailing, in a language Bert didn't know, that he had lost his mother – the reporter's translator had explained this – and all day Bert had heard the boy's wails in the relentless throb of the clinic's air conditioning.

"You look preoccupied." A woman of about fifty whom he'd sometimes seen around the hospital had sat down across from him.

"Tired, I guess," he said.

"Burnout," the woman said. She took a bite of pizza and washed it down with a large swallow of small brewery ale.

Bert shook his head. "Grief," he said. "Mourning. Horror. Nothing to do with the artificial, arrogant concept of burnout."

The woman waved her hand. "Life. Death. Infinity. But you must try not to dwell on it."

"Doesn't it ever overcome you?" Bert said. "Don't you ever feel unassuagable grief?"

"I have a son who channels John Lennon," she said. "I can't afford grief."

"Are you serious?" Bert said.

"Terribly," she said. "We communicate by fax. I'll be standing in the kitchen and the phone rings, and out comes *Imagine there's no heaven*."

"Well," Bert said, "at least it's not Sid Vicious. Do you work at the hospital?"

She shook her head. "Freelance," she said. "I'm a faith healer."

Bert smiled and waited for the punch line.

"Honest to God," she said. "Norton Chestnut." She reached across and shook his hand. "Nondenominational healing through prayer, ceremony and massage."

"This is how you make your living?" Bert said.

"You'd be surprised how many people are willing to pay for a little laying on of hands."

Bert felt himself blush. "What is it you do, exactly?"

"A little chanting, a little prayer," Norton said.

"Um," Bert said, "where do you actually stand? I mean, is this some kind of religion, or what?"

Norton ran her finger back and forth along the edge of the table as she looked thoughtfully at him. "Think of the Psalms," she said. "The beauty of the poetry is inherent, whether you believe in the religion that goes along with it or not."

"And do you?" Bert said. "Believe the religious aspects?"

Norton shrugged. "Words come to me and I pass them on. I'm irrelevant."

"You channel health," Bert said.

"Well," Norton said, "people have needs, and the things I do seem to meet a lot of them." She leaned across the table toward him. "It's not what I believe, but what the patient perceives as truth that does the trick." She sat back. "For instance, if you were my patient, I wouldn't even say 'Bless you' if you sneezed."

"Thank God," Bert said.

Norton nodded. "People like to be touched." She wiped her hand on a napkin and touched his forearm.

Her fingers were cool, but he thought the skin on his arm would burst into flame. His heart began to speed up, and he felt his cheeks flush.

"But what do *you* believe in?" he said.

"Miracles," Norton said.

He watched her fingers drift in slow motion away from his arm, expecting to see their shape branded forever into his skin, and it was all he could do to keep from saying, Touch me again.

Fog had slid into town by the time the crowd left Prevedello's. Bert watched Norton's truck pull away and then plunged into the fog in the opposite direction, his body lumpy with a long-absent but achingly familiar energy. His cheeks felt sharp, as if he had spent the day aboard a sailboat out on the windy bay, and his skin tingled as if all the blood in his body had escaped from his arteries and was racing along just below the epidermis, ready to burst out into the night at the slightest provocation. "What kind of fool am I?" he sang, and he flung out both arms and whacked the back of one hand against a building. "Oh, shit," he hissed, doubling over and clutching it to his chest.

Bert was no stranger to love, but in recent years love had grown strange to him. He was as taken aback by his sudden infatuation with Norton

as he'd been when his mother went off to Alaska
with Michael Crabtree, and the two of them had
called from Homer to say they'd gotten married.

"What do you mean, married?" Bert had
said stupidly.

"It's not as sudden as you think," Bert's
mother said. "I've known Michael for years."

"You were his den mother," Bert said. "Is
this a joke, Mom?"

"I loved your father very much, Bert," she
said. "But I still have a life to live."

There were muffled noises, and Michael's
voice had suddenly blared in Bert's ear. "Hey, Bert.
How's it going?"

"Fine," Bert said. "Have you really married
my mother?"

"I'll tell you something, Bert," Michael
said. "I have been in love with your mom ever
since she went sledding with us on Robinson Hill
after that big storm. Nobody else's mom would
have done that."

"That was thirty years ago," Bert said.

"Listen, I really respected your dad,"
Michael said. "He really had my respect. I could
never fill his shoes."

"He had big feet," Bert said.

"But your mom and I really have
something special," Michael went on. "It's
unbelievable, Bert." He exhaled. "I've really
learned some things from her."

Bert did not ask what they were. But when
his mother and Michael Crabtree had gone back
home to Indianapolis, and Bert had flown out to
spend Christmas with them in their new house, he
was astonished at how fond of each other they
were, and even more at how quickly he got used to

the idea of them being together.

"Life goes on," his mother had said, and he had to admit she was right.

Jason Chestnut was fourteen when he was first contacted by the spirit of John Lennon and told to quit school. "That's what I did," Lennon had said in Liverpudlian tones.

"John Lennon was a dunce with no future," Norton said when Jason reported the conversation at dinner. "He had nothing to lose."

"And a world to gain, Mom," Jason said. "Anyway, he wasn't a dunce. His talent was so great that the world couldn't handle it."

His mother had looked closely at him, no doubt checking him out for signs of drugs, but Jason had gazed steadily back at her. "Did you explain to him that there are laws regarding school attendance for fourteen-year-old boys in this country?"

He nodded. "He said, 'Bloody 'ell. Fuck 'em.'"

"Swell role model you've picked out, Jason," Norton said drily. "How did Mr. Lennon get in touch with you, anyway? By phone, or what?"

"You don't believe me," Jason said softly. "You *never* take me seriously."

"Jayjay, I take you incredibly seriously," Norton said. "I take you more seriously than anything else in the world. That is why I want you to stop this nonsense before you start to believe it."

"I feel sorry for you, Mom," Jason had said. "You would be a lot happier if you could just let it be." Jason had learned a lot about how the world was set up since John Lennon had started talking through him, but his mother didn't want to hear it. She held her mouth in a straight thin line and hardly blinked when Jason tried to tell her anything.

"John says we should forget almost everything about modern technology and spread the message of returning to simpler times," he told her. "Get back to where we once belonged."

"And where might that be?" Norton said.

"Back to the woods," he said. "John says he was Johnny Appleseed and John Muir in former lives."

"And who were you?" Norton said curiously.

"I've been a lot of people," Jason said. "I was the Apostle Paul, and I was Mark Twain, and I was the first AIDS victim."

Norton stared at him. "The first AIDS victim."

"Yup," Jason said. "It was just a very short life, not too long before I was born into this one. I suffered terribly. I was just a little baby."

"This was in Africa somewhere?"

"No, Mom, it was in Maclean, Virginia," Jason said. "Where they developed the AIDS virus. It escaped, and contaminated some embryos they were growing for fetal tissue experimentation. I was one of them."

"Jason, stop it right now," Norton said.

"Oh, fuck, Mom," Jason said. "You are just like all the rest of them. John Lennon has been persecuted all down the centuries."

"John Lennon is dead, Jason, and you are making this up out of your own brilliant imagination," Norton said. "How can I get that through your head?"

Spirit recognized.

Jason smiled. "All you need is love," he said.

In the morning the news from the famine was grim. People with guns were taking the food of people without guns, highly infectious diseases rushed through the refugee camps, and hundreds of human corpses were being bulldozed into the ground every day, but with Norton hovering at the edge of his life Bert's heart was light and his spirits were high.

He was surprised at the remarkable strength of the hope that had seized him. He wished this feeling were a communicable condition, one he could pass along to his patients. He would like to be able to simply touch their wasted arms, hold their sharp faces between his hands and watch their eyes fill with the strange light that he felt in his own cheeks at the thought of Norton. Instead he would have to keep it under wraps; it would be unkind to be so happy in the face of his patients' suffering.

"Open wide," he said to the man on the table before him, and he flashed his light across the ravaged gums that appeared. He knew the lumps and swellings, he knew the look that appeared in the eyes when the symptoms made themselves felt. There might be some reprieves, but there was no escape.

He straightened up and tucked the flashlight into his breast pocket. "We have some choices to make," he said. "Why don't you get dressed, and we'll talk about them."

The young man sighed and nodded.

Bert stepped into the hall, a hard thing that felt suspiciously like a sob lurking in his sinuses. If unshared happiness was detrimental to his patients' well-being, he thought, unexplained grief could be fatal. He went into his office to compose his face.

He was halfway across the room before he realized that Norton was sitting there with her eyes closed and her palms flat on the desk, as if it were about to levitate.

"Oh," he said. "Excuse me." And he began to back up, as if his gears had been suddenly flung into reverse.

"Bert," Norton said, and she opened her eyes.

"Yes," he said, standing still. "Sorry to interrupt whatever you're doing."

"Do I look like I'm doing something?" she said.

"I thought you might be meditating," Bert said.

"I don't meditate," she said. "I think sometimes, but that's about as far as I go. Do you want to have dinner with me tonight?"

Bert felt a rush of hot blood in his ears. "How did you guess?"

"I've got some psychic ability," she said. "I could sense last night that you would be hungry again tonight."

Now the hot blood rushed to his groin. "Huh," he said stupidly.

She smiled and stood up. "I'll be at your place at seven," she said, and she stepped past him and out the door.

Late that night, Bert said into his pillow, "I am healed of all that ailed me."

Kneeling above him, Norton said, "Maybe yes, maybe no. You carry a lot of tension in your shoulders."

"The weight of the world," he mumbled.

"A good image," she said. "Now visualize it as a soap bubble."

He lifted his face from the pillow. "You want me to think of the world as a soap bubble?"

She laughed and ruffled the hair on the back of his head. "Just for the purposes of this massage," she said. "Not forever."

But as he pressed his face back into the feathers, he thought that if everyone in the world could be in love forever, the world might very well *be* as light as a soap bubble. If there was some way of capturing this buoyant feeling, and trapping it in a gelatin capsule, and handing it out for free on street corners, the whole world's tension might dissipate and drift away into the clouds.

Sometimes it amazed Jason that so few people had the capacity to get beyond the limited way society had taught them to think and be open to the wisdom that John Lennon could share with them. He'd thought for a while that it was a generational thing, but then he'd met some other channelers, a woman who must have been forty and channeled Mary Magdalene, and another who told him she was twenty-seven and had been channeling Ping Tsao, a Chinese concubine from the tenth century, since she was seventeen. Channeling made history come alive. It made a big difference if you knew you had been part of things.

Anarcha Entwife, the woman who channeled Ping Tsao, had talked Jason into staying in school until he could legally drop out. "Think of the hassle, man," she said, passing him a joint. "The archaic laws in this country could get you thrown into reform school. It would use up all your psychic energy just trying to survive in one of those places."

"I'm so sick of it, though," Jason said. They were sitting down at the end of the waterfront park, listening to the water lap at the cement dock in the dark, and the wet salt air blowing into his face made his hair fuzz up around his head and his scalp prickle. He felt filled with excitement and grief. He knew he could make a big change in the world's spirit, and he was terrified that he would never get a chance. "I stopped learning anything in eighth grade. I think the real world has more to teach me now."

"Yeah," Anarcha said, and her shoulder brushed his as she nodded her head. "I've really learned a lot since I left home. But you only have another few months till you're sixteen, right? You don't need to make it harder than it needs to be."

"Hey, Jude," Jason said softly. "Don't make it hard."

"Yeah," Anarcha murmured. "That's my job." And she touched him for the first time as she leaned over to kiss him.

"Where will you go?" Norton said.

"I don't really know, Mom," Jason said. He looked over at his mother, who was sitting on his bed with a pair of his socks in her hand, her long blond hair hanging down around her wrinkly face, and he suddenly felt a hot tenderness flow into his throat. His mother had no idea. She knew nothing about him. He rolled up another tee shirt and stuffed it into a side pocket of his backpack. "I'm just going to travel for a while. That's what you did."

"I was eighteen," Norton said. "I'd finished high school. I had plans for the future."

Jason smiled kindly at her. "Kids mature earlier now," he said. He had plans too.

"Couldn't you honor John Lennon's memory by starting a band or something?" Norton said.

Jason laughed. "I have zero musical talent," he said affectionately. "*You* know that. You had to listen to me practice piano." She still thought this had to do with being a fan.

Norton sighed. "Jason," she said. "I can't stop you, I know that. But for God's sake, don't do stupid things. You're so smart. If you sleep with people, use condoms."

Jason knocked his backpack off the bed and onto the floor. "You think I'm still twelve years old."

"No I don't." Norton stood up. "I think you're sixteen and you're too smart to waste yourself. Don't forget these socks." She tossed them onto the bed. "And if you start taking drugs, don't share needles."

"I'm not going to take fucking drugs!" Jason shouted.

"I sincerely hope not," his mother said.

"It's cool for men to cry," Anarcha said. "Ping Tsao says the oceans are made up of the unshed tears of men. Fish are the souls of men who never wept."

"I think it's because I love you so much," Jason whispered. "I can't control myself. It's like a miracle that I'm here with you."

"We were meant to be together," Anarcha said. "No matter how often we get separated, we'll always find each other again."

"That's what I mean," he said. As he wiped his eyes with the heel of his hand he saw three candle flames where he knew there was only one. "It's a miracle."

"Everything in the cosmos is a miracle," she said. "It's just the way it's meant to be."

It was one of the worst winters that Bert could remember. Day after day was muffled with a cold grey fog that hung a few inches above the ground; anyone who stepped outside was instantly chilled to the bone, and the people who lived there were in a chronic condition of hypothermia. The clouds were an impenetrable mass of steel wool, and every passing car carried a solitary, grim-visaged driver. Sometimes, walking along the street in the dim and unpleasant morning light, Bert felt as if he were crossing the surface of a planet whose sun had failed, wading among the bodies of fallen citizens who with their last strength had crawled into doorways and bus shelters as the planet's atmosphere crystallized into ice.

Breathing the thick cold air and tripping around the frosted mounds of blanket huddled on the sidewalk, he couldn't help marveling at what love did to the human psyche. Before Norton showed up in his life, he'd felt as if the cold fog had permeated his skin and filled his entire body up to the bottom edges of his eye sockets; now and then bits of it drifted across his corneas, obscuring the details of the world he was trying to live in. But the day after she appeared – the very minute he saw her! – the sun had burst out and his vision had cleared, and his heart popped up out of the Slough of Despond and had sat bobbing happily in his chest ever since.

It sounded like a severe heart condition. He laughed aloud.

Maybe part of what he'd fallen for was what Norton represented – the idea of hope without dogma, ritual without judgment. If one of his patients believed in God, who was Bert to ignore that path to health? And if someone believed he had been an Indian princess in a past life, why not ask the local Native American shaman to cook up a sweat lodge?

Well, for a number of reasons, not least of which was that he would feel stupid doing it. Besides, he would probably lose his license. Not to mention the type of patient he would attract. Life among the dead and dying was fraught with enough perils without the added burden of flaky patients.

He opened the door to the examining room, smiling at the thought of what Wedge would say if he were to waltz across the room, put his hands on Wedge's head and, with closed eyes, begin to pray.

"You look smug," Wedge said. "Come up with a miracle cure?"

"Nope," Bert said. "No miracles, Wedge."

"Hell," Wedge said, "I wouldn't want one now anyway." Wedge's partner Vinnie had died, and Vinnie's mother had gone back to Wisconsin.

Well, Bert thought as he put his hand on Wedge's neck, you haven't got one. He stood back and looked at Wedge's face.

"You see what grief does to the healthy ones," Wedge said with a bitter smile.

"Treatment is changing every day," Bert said. "We have many options. Don't give up."

Wedge reached up to pat his arm. "I'll do what I can," he said. "But death is really not that scary to me any more."

"Death doesn't scare me, it *infuriates* me," Bert told Norton that evening. "There I am, working like hell to control some stupid opportunistic infection, and I look up to see the ultimate failure oozing through the door like The Blob."

"But you're making progress, aren't you?" she said. "People are living longer?"

"People are *dying* longer," he said glumly. "There's progress, but it's so fucking slow. I wish I could just say no." He jumped up from the sofa and shouted, "No!" crossing his forefingers in the face of an invisible Blob.

"DOC SAYS NO TO DEATH!" Norton said. "THOUSANDS LIVE!"

The phone rang and she answered it, turning her back to him to listen. "Oh, I'd go on taking them if I were you," she finally said. "Finish up the prescription. Sometimes it takes a while. Doctors aren't miracle workers, you know." She laughed. "Of course. I'll do that right now. Call me again in the morning."

"What was that?" Bert said as she hung up, but she held her hand up to quiet him. With one hand on the telephone and her head bent, she stood silently for a long moment. Then she looked up and smiled, and came back to sit beside him.

"Were you praying?" he said, unable to keep the astonishment out of his voice.

"Of course," she said, sounding just as surprised. "I don't lie to people, Bert."

"Who did you pray to?" he said.

"God," she said. "Sometimes people want Jesus, some ask for Mary. And there are Buddhists and Hindus and every now and then a desperate Muslim. Not to mention the ones who want me to intercede with the spirit of the ancient forest."

"What about Satan?" Bert said.

"Nope," Norton said. "No Satanic worship. No praying for harm or evil. Just for help and hope."

"Good motto for your business card," Bert said. He had meant to speak lightly, but it came out sounding mean.

Norton sighed. *"Prayers for help and hope.* That's about right." She patted his knee. "I know you hate this. It will probably be what comes between us in the end."

"I don't hate it when *you* talk about it." He took her hand. "I still don't know what you really believe."

"What I believe," she said, putting her feet up on the coffee table, "is that the brain is more than the sum of its parts. I think it's possible, Bert, that we are little parts of a pattern so large that we can't begin to comprehend it."

"God, you mean," he said, feeling disappointed.

"No," she said, "nothing that simple. I mean that things like ESP, or the Catholic Mass, or the release of endorphins, may be like – " she paused, looking out the window. "The normal phenomena of a system we have yet to discern. A complex ecosystem."

Bert sighed. "What's wrong with good old chaos-based evolution?"

"Nothing," Norton said. "That's just what I'm saying. Chaos-based evolution may not be incompatible with some vast pattern we have no inkling of."

"What about praying? What purpose does that serve?"

"I don't have any answers, Bert," Norton said. "It's just another attempt to understand the universe."

"And what about Jason? What's he doing when he channels John Lennon?"

"Getting attention, getting laid," Norton said. "Changing the world."

Floating naked on his back in the Sacred Waters Hot Spring deep in the Nak-Ne-Tumpqua National Forest, Jason gazed up through the clots of steam and evergreen boughs at the faint stars. From the corner of his eye he could see Anarcha beside him in the black water, her pale blob of a face surrounded by a flapjack of flowing hair. Around them other bodies floated, and at the edges of the pool naked people sat with their feet in the hot water and smoked marijuana. Someone was playing a guitar somewhere in the woods.

They had been in Arizona, hoping to find a Navajo shaman they could study with, when Anarcha had suggested they come up here for a while. "People go there for the winter," she said. "It's like a family."

On the first day his sleeping bag was stolen out of the back of Anarcha's Toyota. They took the back seat out of the car and put an old chenille bedspread on the floor, and at night they huddled there together under Anarcha's bag, their heads up against the front seat and their feet sticking into the trunk. It had been fine sleeping that way the first week or so but lately he woke up cold and cramped, and his brain felt fuzzy for a while in the morning until his neck straightened out and the blood flowed back in.

The pool sloshed and Anarcha's hip drifted against his as someone slid into the water on the other side of her. Jason lifted his head and could tell by the great mound of beard sticking out of the water that it was Gordon, who had showed up at the hot spring soon after they arrived.

"I love you too, Jude," Anarcha had said a couple of hours ago. "I love a lot of people. That's what love is, you know – sharing. It peters out and dies if you try to limit it."

"But I thought we were meant to be together," Jason said.

Anarcha sighed wistfully. "Sometimes I'm with you, sometimes I'm with Gordon. It's this darned eternal triangle. Ping Tsao says it's been my karma through history. Cleopatra, Mark Antony and Julius Caesar. Henry the Eighth and Anne Boleyn."

"I was Henry the Eighth?" Jason said.

"No, I was," Anarcha said. "You were Anne Boleyn, and Gordon was Catherine of Aragon."

"You chopped my head off?" Jason said.

"I felt so bad about that," she said. "I've been meaning to apologize to you for hundreds of years." She slipped her arms around his neck. "I'm so glad you're not jealous this time."

"Oh, sure," Jason said, hoping his voice didn't sound as shrill to her as it did to him. "It's just karma."

Now he lay back in the pool of unshed tears and closed his eyes, and John Lennon said, "You've passed the test."

What test? Jason thought.

"The test of self-sufficiency and cosmic

ability," John Lennon said. "Now it's up to you to spread the word."

I thought I *was* spreading it, Jason thought in surprise.

He could feel John Lennon shaking his spiritual head. "Out here you're preaching to the converted," John Lennon said. "You think Yoko and I stayed in bed for a month among kindred spirits? No way, José. We made sure the world witnessed everything."

I don't know what you mean, Jason thought.

John Lennon laughed. "Think about it, Einstein."

Once Wedge's body had given an inch the disease rushed in to take a mile. His weight dropped away, and at night he tossed in sweat-soaked sheets, envisioning hell and worse.

"I've seen the best minds of my generation destroyed by madness, Bert," Wedge said. "But I never thought it would happen to me."

Bert could say nothing. Let me examine you, let me tell you the options, he thought; keep a stiff upper lip.

"How about those Seahawks?" Wedge said. He touched Bert's hand. "You shouldn't let yourself get so involved."

"There's a new drug," Bert said. "We can get you into a clinical trial."

"No," Wedge said. "No placebos. I want the drug or I want nothing."

"I'll try," Bert said.

Wedge slid off the table and picked up his shirt. "With you and Norton on my side, how can I lose?"

Bert looked at him in surprise. "Norton?" he said. "What's she going to do, pray for you?"

Wedge stopped buttoning his shirt and looked at him. "Somebody has to."

"I didn't mean it that way, Wedge," Bert said.

Wedge shrugged and looked down at his buttons again. "I did," he said. "There aren't any miracles, Bert. You don't have any and neither does Norton. But suppose miracles have nothing to do with it. Suppose it's all *real* up there." He gestured toward the ceiling. "I may need all the help I can get."

"*What's she going to do, pray for you?*" There were implications galore in that sarcastic question, and they were things Bert had no desire to think about – things he had hoped he would never have to face. Falling in love with Norton had been so easy he had hoped that love would solve all their potential problems. He had thought he could separate the woman Norton from the things she did; but did her acts spring from a rational analysis of cause and effect? Was Norton a charlatan? Or did she truly, truly believe what she said?

And would he respect someone who *didn't* believe in what she was doing? Weren't means that took advantage of people's superstitions and vulnerabilities justifiable, if the desired end was reached? Was it right to pray for someone if you didn't believe in the god you were addressing?

As for him – well, it was one thing to tolerate another person's religious beliefs, but just how ethically defensible was it to tolerate the exploitation of those religious beliefs by a third party? Was he, Bert, a shyster himself?

"Wedge was well for so long, I'd hoped he wouldn't get sick," he said at dinner that night. "That's pretty stupid, isn't it?"

"You can't help what you hope for," Norton said.

"I went into infectious disease in the beginning because it had cures that worked," Bert said. "Antibiotics, sugar water. And then here comes this scourge with no cure. It sits there laughing at me, at what a fool I am."

"It's laughing at us all," Norton said mildly. "Can't nobody play God for too long before getting laughed at, Bert."

And Bert supposed that, after all, that's what he'd been doing. He had told himself otherwise; he would have said, if someone had asked, that he had no illusions about his own power over death; but on another level he supposed that the only reason to be a doctor was to make life and death decisions, using his own criteria. A sense of humor, intelligence, skepticism: those were what qualified a person for unending good health and immortality. Anyone else he wouldn't waste his personal time on; but those few – family, lovers, friends like Wedge – he would lie awake over, spend his life on, fight God or Satan for the power to keep alive.

"I have a confession," he said. "I've found myself praying for Wedge lately."

Norton smiled. "It's an automatic response to stress."

"I don't even know what I was praying for," he said. "For time to go backwards or something."

"Most prayer," Norton said, "is really an attempt to deny the truth."

"And yet you do it for a living," Bert said.

"Well," she said, and she reached over to take his hand, "it gets people through the night."

They sat together in the dark, and he remembered sitting with his mother beside his father's hospital bed, after they'd taken him off the ventilator. His father's breathing had grown shallower and shallower, and then a great struggle took place in his chest as at last he was unable to drag any oxygen at all into his corroded lungs. Then, too, Bert had been silently pleading, "Oh please God;" but that prayer, he thought now, was a plea for his own deliverance from the pain of an absurd hope: the crazy and frightening belief that it was in his power to stop his father's dying by just putting out his hand. Plug his father back onto the machines and his father would open his eyes again, and laugh, and reach up to grasp the hand that Bert was holding out.

But he had kept his hand still, and when his father's breathing finally stopped the panic in Bert's chest had flown up his throat into his mouth, where it fluttered until it finally leapt out into the hospital room and was gone, leaving him safe once more in the realm of rational thought, where he had been ever since.

Bert bought a latté and an Italian biscuit of some kind and ate as he walked to the hospital. The morning was cool but not cold and the city had a pent-up feeling, as if spring were some great grief that was about to burst out of winter's reserve. The breeze gusted off the bay and caught in his sleeves, billowing into his jacket. Gulls cried out in sorrow overhead, and the people who lived in the alleys and doorways did not look up as he passed.

Wedge lay flat on his back on the bed, his legs sharp under the light blanket. The slight motion of his chest might have been breathing but might just as easily have been caused by the way Norton was smoothing Wedge's dry, thin hair away from his face as if it was a mass of golden curls.

She looked up as Bert sat down across from her. "He's so tired," she said.

Bert carefully put his hand over Wedge's, which lay on top of the covers, but Wedge gave no sign of noticing.

"He's not in pain, is he?" Norton said.

"I won't let him suffer," Bert said. "I can do that much."

He looked out the window, where he could just see, beyond a hundred roofs, the cold blue bay flashing in the sun. He thought about the last phone call he'd had from his mother and Michael Crabtree.

"Let me give you some advice," Michael had said. "May I? As your stepfather?"

Bert had pictured Michael in his Italian suit, crossing his legs and earnestly leaning forward, and he remembered Michael's father, Mr. Crabtree, a bald and loud-mouthed sort of fellow who would cross his legs and lean forward the same way. Somehow this way of advising had flowed from Mr. Crabtree into Michael and lodged in his limbs and his face and in the future of his hairline, and – with some input from Mrs. Crabtree, of course – made Michael Crabtree what he was now. Bert wondered if the advice Michael was about to give had somehow flowed from Mr. Crabtree, too.

"Age makes no difference," Michael pronounced. "You notice it for the first five minutes and then it never comes up again."

"Thanks," Bert said. "Have you ever thought about channeling, Michael?"

"You mean as a career choice?"

"No, I mean just thought about it," Bert said. "Maybe nothing we think is original. Maybe we're all channeling our fathers."

"I guess I thought that once or twice," Michael said. "When I was about thirteen. Let me tell you something, Bert. I like Norton. I get a good feeling from that woman."

"Vibes?" Bert said.

"Confidence," Michael said. "She's a woman who will treat you right, Bert. A woman who knows something about life."

"Bert?" His mother was on the extension. "*Carpe diem*, dear. That's your mother's advice."

And so he had – he had seized the day. There was no rational reason why Norton should have appeared in Prevedello's that night, or why he should have fallen smack in love with her, or why, despite the difference in their ages and attitudes, they should have stayed together all winter and into the spring; but here they were. He knew a miracle when he saw one.

"Excuse me," someone said, and Bert looked around to see a young woman and a large golden retriever in the doorway. "I do pet therapy? For the dying? Do you think this man would like my dog to visit?"

Bert and Norton looked at each other, and Bert said, "I don't know if Wedge even likes dogs."

"Cats I wouldn't bring if I didn't know," the woman said. "But everyone loves dogs." She leaned over to unclip the leash.

The dog grinned and trotted across the

room, stopping to sniff politely at Bert's thigh before moving over to the bed. He rested his chin on the mattress, and Bert could see the nostrils wiggling as the dog checked out the scene. Then, slowly and more gently than Bert could have imagined an animal that size moving, the dog climbed up onto the end of the bed, one golden foot at a time. He slid his nose under Wedge's hand and began to inch his way up the bed, and at last he lay stretched out at full length, his chin on Wedge's shoulder.

Wedge's fingers began to move, plucking at the dark gold fur.

Bert looked at Norton, sitting there stroking Wedge's hair, and she looked up and smiled at him. He felt, with shame, that he was perfectly happy. If happiness was flowing out of him and down into Wedge's hand, he hoped Wedge didn't mind.

Jason took a carton of chocolate milk out of the dairy case and went up to the counter. "One of those sub sandwiches, too," he said. "And I want to send a fax."

The girl looked at the page he handed her. "Your name is Albert?"

Jason felt himself blushing. "Jason," he said. "That's just a quote."

"Oh," she said. "*The most beautiful thing we can experience is the mysterious*. Cool. To your girlfriend?"

"No, my mom," he said. "It's easier sending her faxes than talking to her."

"Tell me about it," the girl said, rolling her dark eyes.

Jason looked at the name on her little

badge. "Sheba. That's a nice name."

"It's out of the Bible," she said. Holding the receiver to her ear she dialed the number Jason gave her, then pushed a button. The fax machine clicked, and the page started to move.

Jason watched the message he'd printed inch its way in one side of the machine and out the other. He pictured his mother's darkened kitchen, silent except for the hum of the refrigerator, or the furnace fan, if it was a cold night. He imagined the sudden ring of the phone in the darkness, the clicking of the fax machine and the blinking of its little red eyeball, and then his message sliding out as if by magic onto the desk in the corner. He liked knowing that those words would settle down in his mother's kitchen to wait, and be there in the morning when she got up.

NORTH OF MOUNT SHASTA

THE LETTER

When Nora took the letter from Warren G. Menendez, Esq., Attorney-at-Law, out of her mailbox, she frowned, but nothing in his name or the Arlington VA postmark or the sober nature of her name in print – *Ms. Nora Dark* – prepared her for Warren Menendez's message.

Times had changed, Warren Menendez stated. New technologies now made it possible for the government to actually identify who was unknown and who was not. In fact, chances were very good that the body of the soldier from the Vietnam era who lay in the Tomb of the Unknowns could now be identified.

Warren Menendez was able to report that the families of several MIA's had, after years of strenuous effort, persuaded the government to investigate various possibilities as to the identity of these remains. These possibilities had now been narrowed to a dozen.

One of the twelve possibilities was this: the bones of Nora's brother, Lieutenant Henry Beston Dark, had spent the last thirty years in a box under a monument near the nation's capitol.

Did the family of Lieutenant Dark have any desire to join in a petition for exhumation of the body in order for DNA analysis to be performed? To give his family peace and closure at last?

"*Yes, **you**, the family of **LIEUTENANT DARK**, have a chance to win an actual human body!*" Nora flicked the letter with her finger and said into the phone, "Well, I am the entire family of Lieutenant Dark, and I do not want to participate."

"Why not?" Ginger said.

"Dead is dead," Nora said. "Why should I want his body if he's not in it?"

"But you don't have proof."

"If Henry were alive he would have come home," Nora said.

"He might be a prisoner."

"For thirty years?"

"I've heard of it," Ginger said. "I've also heard that there's a whole colony of Vietnam vets living off the grid down around Mount Shasta. They grow marijuana for the medical black market. That's who people are seeing when they report Sasquatch sightings."

"Oh, Ginger," Nora said.

"It's just a thought."

Of course it was just a thought; Henry himself was just a thought. But it *was* rather nice to think of Henry living a Spartan life in a pine bough-camouflaged cabin in the mountains, venturing incognito to a nearby town for provisions, stalking through the snow at the edge of the woods to frighten hunters, curious teenagers, government agents and bounty hunters who sought soldiers absent without leave from the century's wars. She would rather think of Henry alive, growing dope in the wilderness, than lying in a box under a cement slab, the object of millions of tourists' journeys, subjected throughout the rest of American military history to 21-gun salutes, the tread of boots, drums and fifes, and speeches by know-nothing speechwriters out to make a buck. Subject to exhumation, for God's sake.

Henry as Sasquatch! He could do worse.

She said good-bye to Ginger and lay down on the sofa. Dust to dust, ashes to ashes. Surely all dead are unknown, unfound, unfindable. Why petition for evidence that your loved one is gone forever? The evidence is right in front of you: *no one is there.*

Thirty years ago, when her mother called her at school to tell her Henry was missing in action, Nora had stayed in the phone booth at the end of the hall for a long time, staring at the intricate patterns, the loves, the fears, and the predilections that were penned and scratched and carved into the wall. Then she took a deep breath and walked back to her own room, where she leaned against the door, staring at a shoe that was lying half-under her bed, and then went over to the window.

Henry was just coming into the building three stories below.

Nora knew it wasn't really Henry. It was either no one or someone whose hair looked like his; but she ran into the hall and waited, watching the fire door under the glowing EXIT sign. She waited for a long time.

Over the years the expectant feeling slowly disappeared from her chest, but the awareness of what had happened never went away. *Henry is missing, Henry is gone.*

👁 ❤ *NORA DARK*

The first time Nora saw 👁 ❤ NORA DARK scrawled on Black's Bridge she thought she'd misread it. She thought it must be those Satanic runes that get spray-painted on garages and walls – odd pitchforks, little crowns topped by hovering dots. But she turned around, drove back under the bridge, pulled over to the side of the road and craned her neck to look again. There it was, 👁 ❤ NORA DARK, every bit as legible as BLOOD KINGS RULE! or GO COUGARS! or BILLI JO + RAMON = 4-EVER!

She felt as if someone was watching her at that very moment. It was like being stalked.

"It's like GO HOME DOROTHY." Ginger had driven out to look at it on her way home from the hospital and then stopped at Nora's. They sat on the front steps with gins and tonic.

"It's another Nora Dark," Nora said.

Ginger rolled her eyes. "How many Nora Darks do you think there are? I think it's someone from your past."

"Don't be ridiculous," Nora said, though she'd had the same idea.

Ginger put an arm around her. "I bet it's a guy who has secretly loved you for a long time."

"Ginger, somewhere along the line you never grew up," Nora said.

"I know." Ginger swallowed her dregs and stood up. "Well, if you get scared, come on over and play Go Fish. That'll take your mind off your troubles."

"Thanks," Nora said, "but I think I'll be okay."

She waited for something more to happen, but it didn't. No one from the local paper called to

ask her reaction; Sheriff Floyd Peach never
appeared at the front door, notepad in hand,
investigating the mysterious appearance of the
words or the crime of having written them. She half
believed no one at all had written them; a natural
phenomenon like soot or spilled oil had oozed into
a random pattern. It could just as easily have been
the face of the Virgin Mary.

Every now and then she drove out to see if
it was still there. It was like coming to see a lover
who might – even after he's said he loves you –
not show up. There was the row of poplars beyond
the dilapidated barn, there was the sign that said
ONE LANE BRIDGE SOUND HORN. Heart
racing, respiration at a standstill, Nora honked and
rounded the curve.

👁 ♥ NORA DARK.

It was one of the pleasures of her day. It
was like coming home; like being welcomed; like
belonging some place.

Nora had expected great changes to occur
in her life – marriage, children – but when they
didn't, she didn't really notice; the absence of
something that never had been there is hardly a
shock. It was things outside herself that made her
notice her own unchanged condition: the recycling
of fashions from her youth, the children of her
classmates graduating from high school and then
college, the gradual relegation of the war in
Vietnam to history.

The winter her brother was lost, she had
hoped that his girlfriend, Griffin Kimball, would
give birth to Henry's child. Nora was no slouch in
biology, and by her calculations it was just possible
that there could be a child. Of course Griffin, in her

last semester of school, was so busy out in the wilderness and all, she would give it to Nora to raise. She'd come see it at Christmas and its birthday, and in the summer, perhaps, she would take it with her into the field; but Nora would be the one who could provide a home. It would be to Nora that it gave its heart.

But weeks and then months slid by, and no child appeared.

So Nora changed her dream. She saw herself walking the streets of Saigon, peering into the faces of the abandoned offspring of the Americans, until at last she found a little girl with the unmistakable bright grey eyes of Henry Dark. She would hold out her arms and the child would rise up into them to be carried away to a new life. She would turn two, then eight, and be heading into adolescence, before Nora Dark finally let her go.

Then, when Ginger suddenly became a grandmother, years sooner than anyone involved would have preferred, so many of Nora's unacknowledged hopes and losses were stirred up that she felt, for a while, as if it was an event that was done to *her*.

She had never been close to Sierra, but when Ginger told her about the impending baby she had felt a wild flutter in what she supposed was her uterus. She had a silly idea that Sierra would ask *her* to raise the baby. She saw herself pushing a carriage down Market Street, then walking slowly along the same block holding the hand of a stumbling toddler; then she fast-forwarded past a small girl in braids and screeched to a halt far in the future, just as a young woman brought a tiny child into a room in a nursing home to say good-bye to an ancient Nora Dark.

No dice, though. Sierra Jo kept her baby, with nary a thought for Nora's feelings.

Often, now, when Nora answered the phone at night Ginger cried into her ear, "I can't fucking think with this fucking kid screaming." Sierra had a job working nights down at the Silver Slipper, and Omar was suffering the horrible pain of alien teeth erupting in his gums.

"You okay?" Nora said.

"Of course I am," Ginger said. "Sierra didn't sleep for the first four years of her life and I didn't kill her, did I?"

"Want me to come over?"

"Yes," Ginger said, and Nora did. They played cards and drank beer and took turns carrying Omar – who, Nora thought, looked remarkably like a frog – around the house, and joggling him, and giving him soothing things to put in his mouth.

By the time Sierra came home from work he was exhausted, and he was fast asleep before she had held him for ten seconds. She put him into his crib and went whistling down the hall, stopping at the door to say, "He just wanted his mama."

Ginger and Nora looked at each other.

"Snot-nose kid," Ginger said.

THE HABITAT SURVEY

That summer Nora was working for the Forest Agency, surveying the Tumbling Oak timber sale for endangered species, especially Del Norte salamanders. She spent hours crawling through the duff, picking up and turning over rock after rock. In areas that looked particularly good for salamanders – downed logs, rocky streambeds – she set little tin can traps and checked them every day.

Her new bifocals had altered her perceptions. When she reached for things they were not quite where she'd thought they would be; she had to reach with a wider grasp, allowing for more possibilities. She stepped a bit farther when crossing streams. The world was flatter, a touch unsteadier. She walked, she thought, the way turkey vultures fly – with perfect control, but with constantly wobbling wings.

But as her sight worsened, her other senses seemed to improve. That spring she had heard the high-pitched wheezing of nestlings as their parents approached with struggling sustenance, a sound she thought she had lost forever. She could smell the fragrance of the currants that bloom while snow still lies on their leaves and, drifting down from higher elevations, the musky, fetid odor of a sow bear leaving her den for the first time in months. Even her skin was more sensitive, quicker to feel a tick stab the soft flesh beneath her belt or the change in the air around her face just before the sun broke through the clouds.

She was kneeling beside a large nurse log one day, carefully lifting pieces of bark to see what might live underneath, when a voice said, "Shalom." She looked around and saw no one. She sat back on her heels, and from the corner of her eye she saw a man leap into the air from high in a sugar pine. Even as she gasped, though, she saw the line attaching him to the tree as he rappelled his way down the trunk. He disappeared behind a clump of ferns and emerged holding his hand up in what she thought at first was a Vulcan greeting but on closer inspection saw was the signal that had once meant *peace*.

"Beautiful day," he said. He had a vast

amount of hair, much of it in thick, frizzed braids, some of it hanging to mid-chest in a rather straggly beard.

"It is," she said.

He smiled. "I understand you're doing work for the government."

She looked closely at him. "You do?"

He put his palms together and bowed. "I am Shala, a Forest Brother. I have ways of finding out what is going on here."

He *did* look a bit like a forest creature with his wild dreadlocks, his weathered skin.

"You know," he went on, "if you find rare or endangered creatures living in this place, this timber sale will be halted."

"I'm aware of that," Nora said.

The man gazed into her eyes. "If you announce that there are endangered creatures here, it would be an action that would result only in good."

"You mean, even if we find no evidence that any listed species are here, we should claim that they *are*?"

"Exactly," he said pleasantly. "Tumbling Oak, like all of Mother Earth, is sacred ground. We believe that there are certain things that one must do to protect our Mother. These are desperate times, Nora Dark."

He knew her name! but of course it was a matter of public record that she was working on contract for the government. "It doesn't really make any difference what I find," she said. "The Forest Agency doesn't care what the report says, they just have to have it done."

The man raised his forefinger. "It does not make a difference to *them*, but it gives *us* evidence to file for an injunction to stop the sale."

"You would base legal action on information you knew was false?"

"There is no way to be absolutely *sure* there are no listed salamanders here. Ecology is an inexact science."

"But I can't *lie*." Nora was surprised to hear herself sounding like a self-righteous pillar of the establishment. "Besides, it would have to be double-checked. Even if I wanted to, I couldn't fake anything."

He bowed again. "We believe that you have a very old soul. We believe that you will do what is right in the name of our Mother Earth."

"We?" she said. *A Sasquatch colony?*

"The Forest Brothers and Sisters," he said. "We stop what destruction we can, and to the rest we bear witness." He stepped toward her. "There are some who believe that Earth has lost much of her power, the way Samson was said to lose strength when his hair was cut." He shook his head, and his dreadlocks swung like a tangle of bullwhips. "When forests fall, *we* preserve the power they lose; that power walks the earth in us, and when the time comes that the trees rise again, they will find us waiting to return that which is theirs." He salaamed, his head almost on his knees, and backed into the woods, finally stepping behind the very thin trunk of a fir and not coming out on the other side.

For the rest of the project Nora felt as if the Forest Brother and his unseen buddies were lurking in the treetops, peering down on her as she made her way through the woods. To her own disappointment, she could not verify the presence of Del Norte salamanders, or of any listed species.

If an endangered salamander or snail or wolverine was anywhere on the Tumbling Oak sale, it had evaded capture, and she had no evidence to claim its presence.

THE DISAPPEARANCE

Sierra's disappearance stunned everyone, as if they had all walked into a door that no one had even suspected was there.

"I *slept* through it." Ginger said, looking as if she hadn't slept since. "She didn't come home from work Thursday night and I was *asleep*."

"But why wouldn't you be?" Nora said.

"And then in the morning I wasn't worried, I was just mad," Ginger said, as if she hadn't heard her. "I thought she had gone off with Larry again. I thought she had done it on purpose."

"Maybe she did."

"She wouldn't leave her *baby*." Ginger looked at Nora as if she were an alien. "Why didn't I call the police right away? I should have known something was wrong."

Nora was not really surprised. Try as she might, she could not believe that the circumstances of Sierra's disappearance were any more sinister than a desperately unhappy girl running from what looked like unrelieved dreariness. The girl is *sixteen,* Nora thought. Of *course* she ran away. But she did not say this to Ginger, who believed the worst – that Sierra's old boyfriend had murdered her, or that Sierra's father (heartbroken though he *acted*) had kidnapped her, or that a stranger had done to her what every mother fears. Instead she said, "Who are all these people?"

Ginger's dining room table was heaped with piles of xeroxed posters. Beneath the word

MISSING! was Sierra's photo from her sophomore, and last, year of high school, in which she was trying to look sultry; below that it said SIERRA JO BRENNAN, *Age: 16. Last seen at the Silver Slipper Lounge.* Half a dozen women sat around the table folding them into thirds and slipping them into envelopes. One woman typed furiously at a computer keyboard; the phone rang, then rang again, and in the kitchen a fax squealed.

"They brought casseroles," Ginger said. "Every one of them."

They were ladies Ginger knew from the hospital, or from Sierra's schooldays, or from her bowling club, who had all come flooding in when the news of Sierra's disappearance hit the airwaves. In addition, there were people who had lost children of their own, and others who liked being around the excitement and tension of a potential disaster.

The roomful of women bobbed and weaved around Ginger like thick ballerinas, patting her, fetching things for her, firmly making her stay put while they flew from door to phone to kitchen to run her house. Omar wailed from another room but stopped suddenly, and a minute later he was carried in, clean and dry and tremulous. One woman gently moved Ginger over to the sofa and sat her down so Omar could be plopped onto her lap.

"There he is," Ginger cried. "Grandma's sweetie pie."

Omar beamed a toothless smile.

Nora felt like a huge sore thumb. Why couldn't *she* sit beside Ginger on the sofa, hugging her as she always had when men didn't call and jobs didn't come through and Sierra Jo was in trouble again? Something had drifted between them.

"You're Nora Dark!" A grey-haired woman at the dining room table peered at her through glasses that seemed to be tinted green. "For the longest time I thought you were a figment of the imagination."

"I beg your pardon?" Nora said.

"👁 💜 NORA DARK," the woman said.

"Oh," Nora said. "The graffiti."

The woman pushed her chair back from the table, where she'd been putting stamps on a massive pile of envelopes. "*Are* you that Nora Dark?"

"I guess so."

The woman beamed. "You don't know who put it there?"

Nora shook her head. "Probably some student. I substitute at the high school sometimes."

"Well, I suppose it *could* be," the woman said doubtfully. "We should find out! Wouldn't that be fun?" She patted the chair beside her. "I'm Marie Eclair. Here, sit down and help me do this."

Nora sat. "How do you know Ginger?"

"Oh, my, let's see," Marie said. "I temped in Xray once. And you?"

"I've known her a long time," Nora said.

"This is just heart-breaking for her, isn't it?" Marie said. She looked at her expectantly.

Nora reached for a poster and folded it, making Sierra's chin disappear. "It's awful, not knowing."

"Well, we do know some things," Marie said, lowering her voice. "We know that someone in a blue van stopped in the parking lot and talked to Sierra for a long time. And that she got into the van. And that the person driving the van had a gun with him, and that's what he used."

Nora stopped folding. "How do they know?"

Marie looked at her as if she was sizing her up. "If you mean the police, *they* don't know. *They* couldn't find a missing person if she stood in front of them waving the American flag."

"You think she's dead?"

"Oh my yes," Marie said. "Dead, and buried near a lake that's surrounded by very tall trees. That we know for sure."

Nora stared out the window, imagining Sierra walking through the dark parking lot behind the Silver Slipper toward a van where a man with a gun waited. She pictured a lake, the moon rising behind the trees and a cold wind ruffling the surface of the black water. A lost grave.

"One thing you should know, Nora, which most people don't know, including the police. And without which they will get exactly nowhere. And that is the tendency of the universe toward good."

"The universe tends to be good?"

Marie nodded. "When evil happens, it's possible to *feel* the universe straining to set things right. It has an inherent tendency to preserve order. And when that's upset by tragedy, the universe is willing to work with us to resurrect the right way of being."

"It's not God or something?" Nora said.

"God," Marie said carefully, "is a shortcut to understanding the universe. A primitive shorthand for frightened people limited in their capacity to deal with larger, eternal issues. These people want a kind, indulgent parent rather than a wild unknowable universe."

A wild unknowable universe! Nora rather

liked the idea, though she had a little trouble with the concept of its straining to be good. She thought it was quite likely that a wild unknowable universe would let Sierra walk toward a van in the dark and climb in with a man and his gun. A wild universe might even think it's *good* to shoot young women and bury them in the wilderness. To blow up young men and let them die alone in the jungle of a foreign land, as unknown as the universe itself.

"There are some things," she said, "that make me glad I don't have any children."

"My daughter's an attorney," Marie said. "She specializes in custody cases and adoptions. She has many, many contacts."

The front door opened and a huge man stepped in. "Buck Wabash, Search and Rescue." He blushed, if "blush" was the right word for the massive effusion of blood spilling through the planes of his face. "I'm working with Sheriff Peach? We're going to be starting a grid formation search? Behind the Silver Slipper? At two o'clock. Everyone welcome."

Nora watched Buck Wabash back out the door, twisting his hat around in his hands. *Any part of life can be snatched away at any time,* she thought. *The blink of an eye, and all you had based your life on would be gone.* She stood up. "I'm going to help search."

"They won't find anything," Marie said cheerfully, "but it'll make you feel useful."

The Silver Slipper was on the edge of town, the last building in a rundown neighborhood that had once been a cornfield. The street was cordoned off, and the periphery of the parking lot was strung with yellow police tape that read

CRIME SCENE CRIME SCENE CRIME SCENE CRIME. Three or four dozen people stood listening to Sheriff Floyd Peach.

"We'll be covering this area inch by inch," he said sternly. "We'll be searching this field here, walking through yards, checking out garages and sheds, looking into culverts and abandoned cars."

"What are we looking for?" someone said.

"We're looking for anything that could be in any way connected to the disappearance of Sierra Jo," Floyd said. "That could be any item ranging from a purse, or a shoe, to signs of a struggle, to blood or body parts."

A wave of heat slipped from the top of Nora's head onto her shoulders and sank through her to settle like sand in her intestines. Floyd Peach was *serious*. Sierra might be dead. She might be dismembered. She might now be spread over the back roads of the county, a hand here, her severed head staring sightlessly into the treetops. She might be lying in pieces in the vacant lot behind the Silver Slipper. *In a grave beside a lake, under the tall trees.*

"Extend your arms so the person on either side of you is no more than six feet away," Floyd said. "We don't want to miss anything."

Nora found herself next to Buck Wabash in the long line of people who were to sweep the field. He wheezed as they worked their way through the dry grass. "Needle in a haystack," he said. "Teenagers are the worst."

"You do this a lot?"

"Three dead, fifteen living in the last year alone. You find a dead lost child and it kills you. It kills the dogs."

"The dogs?"

"Dogs take it to heart," Buck said, shaking his head sadly. "I've had big alpha dogs just curl up and howl. The one I've got now, coon hound mix is what he is, he just crawls into my lap when he finds your dead body."

"What do you think are the chances of finding Sierra?"

"Well, when you don't hear anything one way or another, there's a good chance that no matter what their intentions were, they get in over their heads. We find them a fair percentage of the time in a condition we wish we wouldn't of." He stopped and pulled a blue bandanna out of his pocket to wipe the sweat from his face. "There is rape. Drugs. Prostitution. Pornography. Murder." He ticked them off on his fingers. "And sometimes the strangest thing is, there is simply forgetfulness. A lack of caring. Anything's possible in the search game."

The search game! It was a vast world of which Nora knew nothing. Places and types of people, kinds of lives and methods of survival, the very hint of which had eluded her for her entire half century of life.

"In this biz, lost kids are a dime a dozen," Buck said. "Half the children in the world have disappeared. Most of the time nobody even notices."

"How did you get started in this?" Nora said.

"It was there in my blood, waiting to be activated by the right teachings," he said. "See, I'm nearly one full part Native American. I'm descended from several tribes. Indians – I call us Indians, I'm not ashamed of that – we can let our spirits wander till they find the lost person, and then sort of look through his eyes to find out where he is. It's a kind of wisdom. White people think it's rare, but everyone has it."

"They do?" Nora said.

"Well, the seeds of it," he said. "It's a lot like cancer."

"Wisdom is like cancer?" Nora said.

"You know, something activates a perfectly normal cell and it starts growing in the wrong place, too fast, all out of whack. If we didn't stop cancer with medicine, or cut it out with surgery, it would spread all through us. Same with wisdom. It starts to grow, and a lot of the time we stop it cold with too much education, or with the strictures of society." He bent over to poke at a Snickers wrapper. Standing up, he glanced at her and away and said, "This Ginger. Is she a child abuser?"

Nora looked closely at his fat red face, gleaming with sweat in the sunlight. "No."

He nodded. "You might not think that's a relevant question, but it is. It might surprise you, but just about every question I ask is relevant to finding this girl."

Nora cleared her throat. "Are you implying that something's wrong?"

Buck Wabash raised his hands in a placating manner and smiled his peculiar smile, which made him look as if he were in pain. "The truth is, I don't think anything foul has happened to her. I believe she's a young woman on the road."

That night Nora lay awake for a long time, imagining Buck Wabash getting his tracking skills activated by his ancestors. How did he do it? Walk around naked in the wilderness, smoking peyote?

Her great-grandfather had owned a gas station. Were gas-pumping skills lurking in Nora's blood, waiting for activation?

She turned over and wadded the pillow up under her head. She felt as if she had stumbled into a parallel universe, where Buck Wabash could look out through the eyes of missing people, where Marie and her friends sat around envisioning murder over coffee. A world where a girl could disappear into thin air.

Like Henry. He had been listed as *Missing in Action* for a long, long time before Nora could admit he was dead. Even now, in a tiny place in her mind, she preferred to see him living in a jungle, drinking green tea, working in a field, teaching small village children to fish. He would have started a library, or become an importer of racing bikes, and he would speed at the head of a herd of bicyclists through the rice paddies on weekends. He would read aloud to his little girls at night before they all climbed into hammocks to sleep.

What if Henry had not disappeared into thin air? What would he ever have been or done? A teacher, a librarian, a bartender? Nothing; he was never meant to be anything. His early death was written in the clouds.

They found a rubber boot, a used condom, a fat and crusty copy of *Das Kapital*, and the desiccated corpse of a cat; but after a week of combing the fields around the Silver Slipper, the neighborhoods on the edge of town, and the woods behind Ginger's house, of Sierra Jo Brennan there was no sign.

NORA'S AURA

Ginger went on *Oprah* and made a damp,

impassioned plea for information while Omar squirmed angelically for the cameras. Afterwards, Sierra was seen in Florida, she was seen dealing blackjack in a casino in Reno, she showed up at the Phoenix airport. She appeared in California more than once – driving down the freeway, tending bar in Union Square, picking up a small girl from a daycare center in Oakland. Every call, every clue was followed up; but none of them came to anything.

Sierra's friends, her acquaintances, and people who had never liked her at all were interrogated, but no one said anything helpful or even suspicious. Omar's putative father, Larry, was politely asked to stay in the state, and investigators called on him at unusual hours and sat in his living room for lengthy periods of time in hopes that he would say something useful. He made one visit to his son and then stayed away. "Don't look like me," he was reported as having said to his friends.

At last the CRIME SCENE CRIME SCENE tape was taken down. More than two hundred people held a candlelight vigil in the parking lot of the Silver Slipper, and the feeling of crisis in the community slowly dissipated. The photocopied posters on the walls of grocery stores and libraries and beauty salons grew tattered and discolored and were covered by layers of posters advertising raffles and lost cats and opportunities to work from home. The volunteer searchers drifted back to their own hometowns.

Ginger went back to work. No more meeting Nora for a beer or to stroll through the mall looking at clothes; she spent her lunch hours with Omar at the day care center, and after work she rushed to take him home, to be ready when the casserole ladies arrived to stuff envelopes and make phone calls.

One night, as Nora sat beside Marie at the dining room table, Marie suddenly pushed back her chair. "Nora, dear," she said, putting her palms firmly on her blue-jeaned thighs, "you know that I am sensitive to a number of qualities. And one of them is, I can sense evil lurking in the good that people mean to do."

"I beg your pardon?" Nora said.

Marie put her hand on Nora's arm. "Nora, this misfortune, this tragedy that has come on your friend Ginger – " It was the first time Marie had ever referred to Ginger as *Nora's* friend. "We feel it emanates partially from you, dear." She squeezed Nora's wrist. "Your aura has become a fog through which we are having trouble seeing. Frankly, if you won't open up to us...well, we will probably never find the missing child."

Nora noticed that Marie's pink lipstick was just a fraction of an inch *beside* her lips, so accurately applied it might have been placed there on purpose. "Do you really believe that?"

"Hon," she said, "it's a surprise to all of us when we discover the power of our emotions and desires. Your time will come."

"But what difference does it make what I believe if Sierra's dead?"

"How can you say that!" Ginger stood across the table from her. Her face looked torn. She had lost weight, despite the plethora of casseroles. "You don't have any idea how I feel. You *can't* know how a mother feels. You don't even care."

"Ginger, just because I don't believe in auras doesn't mean I don't care," Nora said, feeling helpless.

"If you cared you would *want* to believe it," Ginger said. "Nora, I can't do a thing without thinking of my daughter. I don't want to be warm, because she's out there somewhere in the cold. I don't want to lie in my comfortable bed, I don't want to take a hot shower, I don't want to eat or listen to music or even breathe, because maybe – " She choked and started to cry. "Maybe my baby, maybe she can't even *breathe*."

A nearby casserole lady put her arm around Ginger's shoulders and led her out of the room, casting a dirty look in Nora's direction as they went.

Marie said in a low voice, "Even knowing the worst would be better than not knowing." She sighed. "Hon. Something is blocking us from finding the body. It's like when you're lying on the beach and someone steps between you and the sun. You know the sun is there. But all you can see is the shape of the person who is blocking out the light. You need the person to move."

At home, Nora was almost afraid to look in the mirror. Ginger was right; the ragged hole left when Sierra was ripped out of her life meant nothing to Nora Dark. Nora was whole and untouched.

Did Marie indeed have some psychic sense, a way to ferret out some secret, lethal bitterness hidden in Nora's soul? Or was it written all over her face? Marie gave her the creeps; she wanted to just stay away from her. But that would mean giving up on Ginger completely, because Marie and the casserole ladies were always *there*.

Before Sierra disappeared, Nora would have said that she and Ginger were friends for life.

Closer than sisters. That Ginger was the one person in the world who understood her, and with whom she could relax and be herself. So close nothing could come between them.

She had believed that a friend could be your family. She had thought that she herself was the center of Ginger's life; that when Sierra grew up and went away, Ginger would relax into her real life with Nora. But it turned out to be Nora who was dispensable.

She knew Ginger would never see Sierra again. She would raise Omar alone, and Omar, like his mother, would do poorly in school, drop out, probably turn to drugs. Ginger would devote her entire life to raising children to be productive, viable citizens, and she would fail.

The thought filled Nora with despair. Not at the idea of the lost Sierra, the doomed Omar, the failed Ginger. But at the knowledge that all is a matter of luck.

"We make our own luck," Great-grandfather Dark would say, lounging in the doorway of his gas station.

"Nothing occurs by chance," Marie would say, peering over the tops of her glasses.

"We must live in harmony with the winds," Buck Wabash would say.

And Nora? Behind her someone would hiss 👁 ♥ *Nora Dark*, and she would turn quickly around. Or she would not turn around. Yes, that was more likely. She would not turn around at all.

Nora found herself waking early that fall. Usually she lay in bed, waiting for dawn, but sometimes she got up and went for drives as the sky lightened, through woods and hills and down into the valley along the endless gravel roads that ran through the fields. She avoided Black's Bridge. She did not believe that anyone ♥ *ed nora dark,* and she did not want to be reminded of the pleasure she had taken in that stupid mystery. Some skinny brainless freshman biology student had climbed drunkenly over the railing in the night and spray-painted those symbols. And now was in the Army, or in jail, or dead.

She felt as if she had found herself in the middle of her life with no escape. Everything had closed down and narrowed in, and soon it would be winter, the roads wet, the forest floor slick with rotting leaves, smoke curling from chimney after chimney. The very birds at her feeder were furtive and indifferent. She was glad there was no demanding, whining daughter to feed or drive anywhere, no one to argue about lipstick and pierced body parts with, no one growing up to hate her. No one growing up to disappear from her life.

Then, on a cold October night, she flipped on the television to find Griffin Kimball glaring at her. In recent years she had become quite famous, and Nora saw her from time to time on the news or on nature documentaries, a skinny woman with close-cropped yellow hair angrily denouncing the deterioration of the natural world. *My sister-in-law,* she always thought, because Griffin Kimball was the closest thing to a sister-in-law she would ever have.

"They're going to finish up on this continent within two years, and in ten they'll have wiped out every last giant in Siberia," Griffin said now. "If we don't stop them they'll cut down every ancient tree on the planet."

The camera switched to the reporter. "What

steps have you taken, Dr. Kimball?"

"We're going after them," Griffin said, and the camera flashed to her clenched fist. "We have a dozen actions going, and lawyers working around the clock."

"Dr. Kimball, how much support do the Forest Brothers and Sisters really have?"

"The American people are behind us," Griffin said. "Not to mention the population of the world."

A man leaned in front of her and said, in a voice so soft it could barely be heard, "Tumbling Oak is sacred ground." It was Shala, the Forest Brother who had asked Nora to lie.

The reporter reappeared on the screen, struggling to keep her hair from blowing across her eyes. "Do you really think you can stop them?"

Griffin Kimball smiled grimly and crossed her arms over her chest. "Or die trying."

"Dr. Kimball, what about the girl in the tree? Isn't her very life at risk?"

Griffin started to speak, but a hand shot into the picture and grabbed the microphone, and the camera quickly focused on an angry-looking young man with a shaved head.

"You guys just don't get it, do you," he said fiercely, a muscle in his jaw popping as he spoke. "The life of this entire *planet* is at risk. With every tree cut we come *that much* closer – " He held up his thumb and forefinger, a fraction of an inch apart. "– to *annihilation*." In the other hand he held up a cell phone. "Ask *her* why. Ask someone who is risking her life to try and save the world. *Ask* her."

The camera panned the faces of the protesters until the reporter said, "We're patched in now," and it zoomed in to focus on the forest canopy behind them. In the upper corner of the screen appeared an inset photograph of a rather sultry young woman's face.

A voice – apparently that of the pictured girl – said, "I just want to do everything I can to save the earth."

In her living room, holding a warming can of beer, Nora felt as if the world had slipped out of orbit, casually tossing her from its surface as it went. A roaring sounded in her ears, and in it she heard the wild, unknowable universe laugh.

THE FOREST ACTION

Tumbling Oak was gone. Oh, the trees were still there; but the living silence of the forest, the rustling of its leaves, the scurrying of small beasts in the duff, were lost in the important comings and goings of human beings and their vehicles. Nora's truck, winding its way up the dusty roads, followed half a dozen cars and was followed by more.

At the turnoff onto the last gravel road a fierce yellow sign warned AUTHORIZED PERSONNEL ONLY, but no one stopped. A mile or two farther along was a new clearing filled with heavy equipment – a bulldozer, some culvert pipes and a heap of plastic tubing. The timber company was about to make the cut. Nora's traps had caught only mice and fence lizards, and she had been unable to stretch what truth she had found. She had done nothing to prevent Tumbling Oak from being razed.

She parked behind an old Datsun whose passengers were pulling sleeping bags and a cooler from the trunk and followed them up the road between dust-covered cars proclaiming COWS KILL SALMON or BIOPHILIA LIVES! or 👁 ❤ MY COB HOUSE on their bumpers. At the top of the hill they came to a barrier of cars, trucks, sheet metal, a refrigerator, and logs on top of which sat a young man, feet dangling and a cell phone to his ear.

"Friend or foe?" he called, and when the woman from the Datsun cried *Friend!* he grandly waved them around the side.

On the other side of the barrier people stood in dusty little groups, talking and laughing, while two women in bright saris danced in the center of a circle of young men beating drums.

"In on the kill, I see."

Nora turned to find Griffin Kimball watching her.

"Hello, Griffin." To her surprise, she had a lump in her throat. She had last seen Griffin in person nearly thirty years ago, but over the years the TV camera had been neither kind nor unkind to her; it had been perfectly accurate. Griffin was still skinny; the thick lenses of her glasses did not obscure the cornflower-blue eyes; her strawlike hair was neither shorter nor longer than it had ever been, nor had its style altered in the least from the Prince Valiant cut she had always worn.

"Here to gloat?" Griffin leaned toward her. "Feel the preternatural silence, the calm before the proverbial storm, Nora? We're waiting for the fireworks to begin."

"A lot of people," Nora said, looking at the dancers. "What's going on?"

"The governor's shutting us down. The National Guard is on the way."

"But why?"

"Well, you see, Nora," Griffin said, speaking slowly and loudly, as if she were a small and not very intelligent child, "they want to cut down the trees, and we have no legal way of stopping them. No thanks to you. But we won't get out of their way. Ergo." She raised her eyebrows. "If you didn't come for the showdown, why *are* you here?" She pulled one of her nasty little cigars from her shirt pocket and lit up.

From her own pocket Nora took a poster and unfolded it. **MISSING!**: Sierra Jo Brennan, Age: 16.

Griffin looked at it without touching it. "Somebody you know?"

"My friend's daughter," Nora said. "We've been looking for her for months. The police, the FBI."

Griffin pulled at her cigar, turned her head and blew a cloud of smoke into the air. Then she sighed. "I *asked* her. If there was anything we should know."

"Posters have been up everywhere," Nora said. "Didn't you see them? Didn't you see it on TV?"

"I don't watch TV." She looked past Nora and shouted, "Daniel!" When a thin bearded boy in jeans two sizes too large ambled over, Griffin seized the poster from Nora's still-outstretched hand and thrust it at him. "Did you know about this?"

Daniel glanced at it and shrugged. "I figured it was her business. There's no law against leaving home, is there?"

"There are laws about statutory rape," Griffin said, flicking her finger violently at *Age: 16.*

Daniel looked at Nora. "Are you a cop?"

"I'm a friend of her mother's. Who is at home taking care of Sierra's little boy."

"She has a *kid*?" Daniel said. "Man, she never told us she had a *kid*."

Griffin hurled her cigar down and ground it out under her Vibram sole. "Damage control time."

"Look," Nora said, "let me talk to her. What tree is she in?"

"She's not *in* the tree any more," Daniel said. He snickered.

Nora looked from him to Griffin. "Where is she?"

Griffin grinned. "The best laid plans," she said. "First thing this morning we took her in to South Valley Hospital."

"Good lord," Nora said. "What happened?"

"A very bad case," Griffin said, "of poison oak."

If Nora had been nursing a not-so-secret hope that she would be the one to find Sierra and return her safe and sound to her mother, she was defeated in that hope by Ginger's health insurance. Sierra's skin was covered with rash, her entire body had swollen until she was almost unrecognizable, her temperature was raging and her breathing was labored, but when the emergency room doctors decided she should be admitted, a woman from the business office insisted on proof that someone would pay for her stay.

The Forest Brother who had brought her in was frantic. "We'll *pay*," he said again and again. "We'll take up a collection."

But even Sierra, ill as she was, could see that the woman wasn't impressed by the vision of

the Forest Brothers and Sisters passing the hat.
"Shala," she whispered, "call my mom down in
Xray. I think I'm still on her insurance."

Your friends may be your family, Nora
thought when she heard this story, *but when it
comes to health insurance, it's blood that counts.*

On the day Sierra was released from the
hospital, Nora went over to welcome her home.
When she walked in she found Marie and Ginger
on the sofa, watching Sierra and Omar play on the
floor. Sitting cross-legged beside them was Shala.

"He brought food up for me," Sierra said,
putting her arms around his neck and snuggling
against him. "And CD's and things so I wouldn't
get bored."

"It's important to keep up the tree-sitter's
morale," Shala said. "The only way to make a long-
term change in the world is by paying close
attention to the short-term details."

"Think globally, act locally," Sierra said.

"I feel just like butter," Ginger said. "Like
I'm getting dents wherever anyone touches me. I
think I could melt."

Marie patted her shoulder. "You are so
open to everything right now. You're in contact
with some very great spirits. Also, your defenses
are down. If you're not careful you may get a cold
or something."

"I bet that's why my poison oak got
infected," Sierra said. "I was so depressed that the
trees were going to be cut. My defenses were
down."

"Hon," Marie said, "I just want to know,
how did you get poison oak in a *tree*?"

"It grows there," Sierra said. She leaned

back on her hands, stretching her legs out in front of her. "That tree is so huge, *everything*'s up there. Things growing on the branches, like even roses, and blackberries, and there was this one little sort of pool full of water, where a branch had broken off. And there was this little mouse that came and drank out of it."

"Yuck." Ginger made a face.

"A little red mouse, about so big." Sierra held up her fingers. "I think he lived up there, and the little pond was where he got his water."

Nora frowned. *A little red mouse?*

"You've gotten so *big* while Mommy's been gone," Sierra said, accepting a pretzel stick from Omar. She patted his bottom as he headed back to get another one.

"You've been away from him for a long time," Ginger said. "It's going to take a while before he's sure you're his mother."

"Oh, he knows who I am," Sierra said a little impatiently. She sighed. "My life is so changed. It's like I have a real commitment to something now."

"You mean Omar?"

Sierra rolled her eyes. "Well, sure. But now I have something to do with my life. And people who don't sit around *judging* me." She gave one of Shala's braids a playful tug. "We're going to be living in the Forest Brothers and Sisters intentional community."

Shala casually put his hands on his knees, palms up, and lightly touched the tips of his thumbs to the tips of his third fingers. He smiled at Ginger.

"You're planning to get married?"

"We don't *believe* in marriage," Sierra said.

"Our community has a commitment ceremony adapted from Druid and Lakota beliefs," Shala said. "It's a far deeper commitment than the conventional Western marriage vows."

"Well, that's very nice," Ginger said. "And what will you be doing after you make this commitment?"

"Mom, I just *told* you, I'm an *activist* now. We're saving the ancient forest."

"And what about Omar?"

"He'll be *fine*," Sierra said. "He'll have *lots* of mommies, and daddies too."

"You're not taking that baby anywhere," Ginger said.

Sierra laughed. "Mom, don't you think you're getting just a little bit possessive here? *I'm* his mother."

Ginger leaned forward. "You chose to leave him."

"But I've come back now."

"Too bad," Ginger said. "You were gone a long time, sweetie. I've been to court. I have legal custody of Omar."

Nora glanced at Marie, who smiled back. *My daughter's an attorney. She specializes in custody cases.* "But he's my *son*," Sierra said. "I left him with you temporarily."

"If you try to take him off to some commune," Ginger said, "you'll *never* get him back."

Sierra stared at her mother open-mouthed for several seconds. Then her face twisted and she burst into tears. "You are *sick*," she hissed. "Let's get out of here, Shala. I'll get my stuff." She scrambled to her feet and stomped from the room.

Ginger jumped up and ran after her. With a

piercing shriek Omar stumbled along behind.

"Poor, innocent baby." Marie said, and she too disappeared into the hall.

"Shala," Nora said in a low voice, "I don't remember tree-dwelling mice in the Tumbling Oak inventory."

Shala, who had closed his eyes when Sierra left the room, opened them.

"A tree-dwelling mammal *could* have been missed," Nora said. "It might not have come down low enough for any of my traps."

He nodded, his eyes on her face.

"There are several tree-dwelling voles," she said carefully. "It could be any of them. But it would most likely be the red tree vole. If someone found *Phenacomys longicaudus* on Tumbling Oak it could be significant."

"I'll find one," Shala said. His pupils had widened until his eyes were black; he spoke so seriously he might have been making a vow of eternal commitment.

Sierra rushed into the room clutching a stuffed canvas bag from which the arm of a sweater swung wildly. She seized Shala's hand and jerked him to his feet, then turned toward her mother, who was carrying the snuffling Omar. "You can't take a baby away from his mother."

"You start taking some responsibility," Ginger said. "Then we'll see who qualifies as his mother."

"You're a *terrible* mother," Sierra screamed. With her eyes squeezed into slits and her face contorted with fury she looked startlingly similar to the baby she'd been sixteen years ago, who would rather *die* than sleep. "I'd rather have *anyone* for a mother than you." She stepped over and leaned close to Omar. "Don't you cry, baby boy. Your mama's coming back for you as soon as she can." Omar hid his face against Ginger's shoulder. "Come on, Shala."

Shala bowed to Ginger and Marie, then turned and bowed to Nora. As he raised his head he winked at her before he followed Sierra out the door.

"Enjoy your fucking commitment ceremony," Ginger shouted.

Marie joined Nora at the window to watch Sierra and Shala get into the old blue van. As it pulled away an arm shot out the window, middle finger extended.

Marie shook her head. "Thank God there's no media here for *this*."

THE KNOWN SOLDIER

Sometimes, in idle moments, Nora would imagine how she might have felt if the last letter from Warren G. Menendez, Esq., Attorney-at-Law, had contained different news. Suppose it *had* been Henry in the box under the cement slab? Would she have been *required* to move him?

But the letter from Warren G. Menendez – well, it was the news she would have chosen: the Unknown Soldier was someone else's brother. Someone else's brother had been dug up, his DNA tested, and his remains taken back to Iowa or Little Rock or western Texas. Someone else's tiny, hidden, unacknowledged hope was gone forever.

Henry was where he belonged: missing.

He could still be Sasquatch, tending his crops in high mountain clearings, ducking under the trees at the sound of helicopters.

He could be leaning back as evening came

on in Ho Chi Minh City, smoking a pipe, telling a little granddaughter about his long-ago childhood in a foreign land, and about his big sister, Nora, who had loved him and taken care of him until he had to go away to war.

"You look like her when she was a little girl," he would say. "You look just like your Great Aunt Nora."

And the granddaughter, gazing in the direction of the setting sun, her eyelids heavy with sleepiness, would put her hand against her grandfather's chest to feel the slow comforting beat of the heart inside, and think *No Ra Dark. No Ra Dark. No Ra Dark.*

THE WILD UNKNOWABLE UNIVERSE

On a warm autumn day, Shala helps Nora climb into the saddle, tighten the webbing across her hips, set the steel ring of the ascenders into the link and screw it closed. "This is as safe as can be," he says. "You cannot fall." He shows her how to tie her shot pouch onto the throwline.

She tosses the line twice, then hooks it over the lowest limb of the fir on the third try; she pulls the climbing rope over the branch, secures it, and sets the ascender on the rope. She puts her feet in the stirrups and sits back in the saddle.

"Lift your knees," Shala says. "Then stand up."

Nora sits, raising the lower ascender, then stands and raises the upper ascender; sitting, raising, standing, she lifts herself into the tree.

It is a Douglas fir, probably 300 years old, and its branches are buried inside mats of lichen, its bark thick and rutted. The cool air is as dense as the lichens, and every sound is softened. Nora

hears Shala coming up behind her on the other side
of the tree, the soft click and whir of the ascenders
as they slide up the rope and a tiny snap from one
of his knees every time it bends.

 She sits on a branch and secures her safety
strap, then unhooks the ascenders, tosses the
throwline and pulls the rope over a higher branch.
When it's resets she releases her safety strap and
climbs again. When she finally reaches the small
wooden platform tucked into the crotch of a limb
snug against the trunk where Sierra spent the
summer of being lost, she fastens the safety line to
her saddle and looks around.

 The platform is only two-thirds of the way
up the tree, but it's high enough that she can see all
of Tumbling Oak and the surrounding mountains
spread out below. The bare hillsides are
crisscrossed with the mesmerizing pattern of trails
created by generation after generation of black-
tailed deer. Minuscule trucks inch along dirt roads.
Here and there she sees gleaming stretches of the
river as it winds west through its watershed.

 She turns slowly, looking through the fir's
branches at the jumble of ragged, cut-over
mountains. Ravens cross the sky in pairs, a jet
streaks by leaving its mysterious smoke-signal
wake, and suddenly Mount Shasta appears, floating
on a pale cloud far to the south.

 On a large limb, not far from the hollow
where water collects, Shala had set the pitfall trap
in which he caught a bright cinnamon-colored vole
with a silvery gray abdomen and a black tail. It
was the red tree vole, Phenacomys longicaudus,
and although it is not an endangered species it is a
species of special interest to the Forest Agency, one
that must be managed for, and around whose

homes and habits the Forest Agency must rearrange its activities, including the cutting of trees. The Tumbling Oak timber sale must now remain uncut while its ancient firs are inventoried and searched and the presence of P. longicaudus *verified and quantified. Tumbling Oak has been taken off the market for the foreseeable future – an admittedly short time, but all that people can manage. Perhaps it will be long enough.*

Safely secured to the old fir, Nora leans over to peer into a mass of twigs, the abandoned nest of an owl. Another, smaller nest is constructed on top of it. It is the nest of a red tree vole.

She inches over to kneel beside it. At one edge is a smooth twig a little larger than the rest, marked with delicate scratches, little etched lines that seem to form a pattern. It's a tiny graffito, its runes and letters so fine that perhaps no one else in the world would recognize them. But even before she lifts her chin to squint through her bifocals, Nora Dark knows what it will say.

👁 ❤ Nora Dark.

ONE OWNER, RUNS

God is really only another artist.
– Pablo Picasso

When John Wayne Turner lost his eye in the woods he lay for a while on the ground waiting to die. The sow who had taken the whack at him scrambled noisily out from under the tree trunk into the clearing. She snorted, and prodded his legs with her nose, but apparently she wasn't hungry enough to taste him, for after huffing threateningly she crashed away through the dead leaves.

He was surprised at how clearly his mind was working. When he'd felt the long claws deep inside his head he was sure they'd plunged into his brain, and after the bear left he lay trying to remember which hemisphere did what, and what sort of disability would result from the loss of half a brain.

Then he was walking carefully down the hill toward camp, pressing his wadded-up felt hat against his head to hold in what was still there. He was amazed at himself – that a man who perhaps had little left but one eye and a brainstem could negotiate the downward-plunging trail, could notice, through that one remaining eye, the brilliant red of the poison oak, and could hear – *He still had an ear!* – the cheerful, encouraging notes of the chickadee that flitted through the trees at his side, keeping him tiny company.

As he walked, the whistling chickadee was joined by more chickadees, and then by a silvery chorus of what must have been golden-crowned kinglets; John Wayne was afraid to move his one eye toward the sound for fear of spilling his gray matter. But the sound grew louder and stronger, and he suddenly realized he was surrounded by a bevy of tiny singing angels! These quick-hearted birds were surely the true messengers of God, carrying small brave cries of hope to the afflicted.

When Caspar Wing dropped dead in the middle of a polka at his fifty-fifth high school reunion, Ruth was, of course, shocked, but she wasn't really surprised, because Cap had had a bad heart for some time and could have gone at the drop of anyone's hat. In the ensuing hubbub she heard one of his classmates mutter, "Damn fool, dancing at his age," and she silently agreed.

"Why not go out in the middle of a good time?" he always said before he did something foolish. She hadn't known why not before, but now she did: when you die in public you ruin a lot of other people's good times.

She followed the ambulance guys across the gym as they trundled Cap's lifeless form away, then turned at the door to look back. At the sight of the white faces of Cap's surviving classmates, she called, "Go on dancing!"

The mouths of several faces dropped open.

"Strike up the band!" she cried. "He would want it that way!"

But the life had gone out of the party as fast as it had gone out of Cap, and an elderly woman with red hair put her arm around Ruth's shoulder and turned her away. This infuriated Ruth, but she let the woman walk her outside, where another of Cap's ancient classmates, who had been a lawyer during his real life, eagerly began to explain the procedures from here on out.

The only thing Ruth Wing had ever wanted other than life with Cap was solitude. She wouldn't have changed anything about the past; she loved Cap, and they enjoyed being together. But sometimes she had felt that just as she was soaring into the universe, Cap was retracting. When she first began to gain a small reputation with her painting, he insisted that he was proud of her work; but every time she came out of her studio feeling exhilarated, or pleased, or even puzzled by what she was doing, he was waiting for lunch.

She never wished Cap gone, but she had always thought that, *if* he were to go first, she would finally have some privacy; she would see what flowed from her unimpeded, uninfluenced by the presence of a husband.

But no one would leave her alone. For the whole time she was in Chicago, Cap's old girlfriends pawed at her, and on the plane home the stewardess got wind of her bereavement and hovered over her in a most irritating way.

And when she finally walked into the terminal, there was Guy. Deep troughs ran from the sides of his nose to the corners of his mouth, and so much of his forehead was exposed that it looked as if the weight of his ponytail had pulled his entire scalp backwards. *What a Sad Sack!* she thought, and with a shock bigger than the one she felt when Cap dropped to the floor, she realized her son was a middle-aged man.

She made her way through the crowd and he put his arms around her. "I never even knew Dad could do the polka."

"Well, he grew up in that Polish neighborhood," she said into his shirt, and finally she started to cry.

Once the excitement of getting Cap buried had died down, Guy showed no signs of leaving. He went out every day, coming home hours later with his BMW covered with dust, and she knew he'd been driving aimlessly around in the woods, the way he always had. After washing the car, he'd drift inside and disappear upstairs with a beer.

Guy had been a poet in his youth, but lately he was selling cars in Beaverton. "Not just *any* cars, Mom," he had told Ruth. "Beemers. Cream of the cream."

"I wish you'd go back to poetry," she'd said.

"These cars *are* poetry. The shine of them. The wind in your hair, your baby pulled up snug into your armpit, your hand on the stick."

"Give me a break, dear," Ruth said.

"Anyway, look at the poets who made their livings outside the academy," he went on. "Stevens, Williams, Larkin."

"And the heroes of literature who sold cars," Ruth said drily. "Rabbit." She sighed. "I wish you were happy."

"Some people are never happy," Guy said, "and I'm one of them."

Ruth had left it at that. She supposed that
Guy's commitment to poetry had never been
particularly deep. He had been married once, many
years ago, and she suspected that the failure of that
marriage was part of what had drawn him away
from poetry. She didn't blame him, really; poetry
and marriage both open you to vast uncharted
worlds, and if one slapped you in the face, you
might well close yourself off from the other.

She looked across the table at him, holding
his coffee cup in one hand as he read the morning
paper, his vast forehead wrinkled, his hair gray and
uncombed. Just when you get out from under the
burden of marriage, she thought, you discover that
you will always feel responsible for the happiness
of the child you brought into the world.

What Guy had not told his mother was that
one morning, not long before his father died, he
had awakened with the terrible fear that he was
Jesus Christ.

He lay in bed, his heart pounding. If it was
true – and he had no reason to think it wasn't –
he'd done everything wrong so far. The memory of
every time he'd ever hurt anyone came flooding
back to him as he stared nearsightedly at the
ceiling. He couldn't even think without yet another
of his stupid mistakes and mean acts suddenly
looming up from the dark regions of his brain. This
had happened to him before – an inability to think
of anything good, or even neutral – but that
morning it was as if a film of his entire life was
running in an endless loop before his eyes as his
poor brain attempted to re-envision himself in the
light of his revelation.

He stayed in bed for a long time pondering

the logistics. Had he been Jesus Christ since he was born – a reincarnation, maybe? Or had he descended during the preceding night to possess the body of Guy Wing? Who seemed to be unchanged; it was, after all, Guy Wing's memories that were making him feel so depressed.

He closed his eyes and saw nothing but blackness. If this was some kind of flashback it was certainly a sober one – no colors running into each other, no glitter along the edges of his eyelids, no voices.

He wasn't sure what to expect. For all he knew he had a halo that would show up in the sunlight. He imagined himself moving in slow motion down the road, dogs and children tagging along, birds alighting on his shoulders. The things he touched would turn to gold; when he leaned over to drink from a fountain the water would turn into wine.

But when he finally left the house, nothing unusual occurred. At the grocery store no one stared at him in the parking lot; no one dropped their pickles or fell to their knees as he walked through the aisles. When he wrote out a check and the clerk asked for ID, he thought for a split second of just flashing his palms, but his only scar was the place on his finger where he'd burned himself with a sparkler forty years ago. So he handed the clerk his driver's license, and she wrote down the number without even looking at his face.

A week went by, then another, and Guy waited patiently, but his conviction that he was Jesus Christ remained tucked into him – not quite in his brain, but not deep enough in his viscera to be ignored. He was constantly aware of it. If he was now Jesus Christ – whether he always had been, or had just turned into him, or, perhaps, was only being *borrowed* by him – if he was Jesus Christ, what was he supposed to do? Surely he shouldn't be selling cars. How did Jesus spend his time? Doing carpentry. Holding suffering little children on his lap.

Then, suddenly, Guy's father died – his regular, flesh-and-blood father. He took a leave from the dealership and drove south, weeping. When he got to his parents' empty house he carried a six-pack of beer upstairs and lay on his old bed, lifting his head now and then to take a drink.

He got up late in the afternoon, in time to go to the airport to meet his mother. At the sight of his reflection rising into the mirror above the bureau, he went closer and stared at himself. He looked like an old man. He looked exactly like his father.

What Kyle Bodine liked about being Outreach Pastor at Your Friend In the Vale was the way it let him slide right into a person's life. Even when he was still in Bible College, if he was to walk into a room where people were having difficulties, they turned to him eagerly, their faces wet, a kind of light shining from their gleaming cheeks. At the sight of him their mouths opened, just a bit, and he could *see* the darkness from their souls, smiling blackly and daring him to bring them to Jesus.

On his way to make calls up in the hills, Kyle would concentrate on envisioning Jesus' love going out to warm troubled families. He pictured it as flooding over a dam, like the one that lay across the top of the valley and kept back the cold waters of the mountain wilderness. People could swim in the man-made lake of those waters all they wanted, but they had experienced nothing like the flood of Jesus' love that would occur in the latter days, when the dam would be taken down.

When he had that vision, he pulled over to the side of the road and wrote it down in his daybook. He would preach on it one of these days.

Corbett Hildebrand was the Head Pastor at Your Friend In the Vale, and Kyle never got tired of listening to him preach.

"I never stopped walking with the Lord," Corbett would say, "but man, he took me the long way around."

The congregation would laugh, knowing what was coming.

"Our Lord led me over hill and over dale," Corbett would say, and he would start to pace, as if the Lord was leading him back and forth across the stage. "You know these things we hear on the television night after night? Wrong living?" He would stop and look out at the congregation, and they would nod, encouraging him. "Man, you know I'm talking drugs. Alcohol. Welfare. Abortion. *Lye*-centiousness."

He would bow his golden head over the microphone. Then with a jerk, as if the Lord had seized his shoulders and shaken him, he would straighten up and begin again to pace. "The Lord has shown me these things first hand, my friends. Yes!" He stopped, turned toward them, and flung wide his arms. "I've gotta tell you, people, I have walked down these mean streets among these sinful temptations, and I have been tempted, and I have given in!" He pulled the microphone close to his mouth, like Mick Jagger, and whispered, "I *know* these sins. Because I have committed them."

At these moments Kyle could feel a lessening of available oxygen as the hundreds of congregants in the tiers around the stage sucked in their breaths in horror and delight.

"Look at me," Corbett would whisper, and sometimes he would sink to his knees like Elvis, holding the microphone with both hands. "Look. At. Me." He threw his head back and knelt exposed before them, a couple of buttons open on his shirt, his very soul defenseless.

Someone in the audience made a sobbing noise.

Slowly Corbett would raise his head, sit back on his heels, and bring the microphone back to his lips. "My Lord took me to the depths," he would whisper, "and let me climb back out again, because He loved me. And He loves you. Oh, man, you can't believe how much the Lord loves you!"

He would get to his feet, walk over and sink into his chair, one arm hanging down at his side, as if he were exhausted. He would whisper into the mike, "If you think you know love, wait until you have experienced *His* love."

A warm wind rolled toward the stage as the crowd let out its breath.

"How did you learn to preach like that?" Kyle had asked. "You really pull them in. You know right when to pause, and when to shout, and everything."

Corbett just shook his head. "Kyle, when I'm up there, it's the Lord talking. Half the time I don't even remember what I've said."

At first Kyle did not believe him, but he saw it happen again and again, Sunday after Sunday. It was too intense, and Corbett was too drained and exhausted afterwards for it to be an act. It was the truth.

Kyle wished he had gone through the things Corbett had. He wished the Lord had spent more time with *him*.

After the raw edges of his face had healed and his mouth was again able to form words, John Wayne would tell his story at dinner parties.

"Angels?" someone would say. "That doesn't sound like you, John Wayne."

"Oh, I think it does," another said. "Faith lies right under our skin, and at the first incision it erupts to color our perceptions."

"Faith can be beaten *into* you or released *from* you," said another. "The next thing we know, John Wayne will be proselytizing in his lectures and hiring missionaries as field assistants."

And amid much laughter the hostess would offer more wine, and the conversation veered into another channel.

What John Wayne did not say at dinner parties was that, as he stumbled through the woods, he had felt an arm slide around him, and he had experienced such relief that he at once gave up all attempts to control events and allowed himself to be guided down the steep hill to the place where his life could be saved. In fact, what he had relaxed into felt exactly like the warm embrace of God.

But why God? Why not think, *My instinct, advanced education, subcortical action, and the ability of the body to continue to function under stress will lead me safely home?* No, at the moment of stress his primitive brain had sprung to the fore and conjured up a god who walked him back to camp as if he were a child.

Corbett said that even if people didn't actually come to worship at Your Friend In the Vale proper, it didn't mean they wouldn't accept the Word if it was delivered to their doors. He held that an effective Outreach Pastor would show up right before dinner.

"Breaking bread with someone puts you on the fast track to their heart," he explained. "Call down the blessing of Jesus in someone's own kitchen and they can't help but feel an obligation to listen to you."

But Kyle felt uncomfortable showing up at mealtimes, so he carried a sandwich in the car, and when he started to get hungry he would turn onto a side road and park with a good view of a valley or of distant snow-covered peaks and eat his lunch alone, pretending he was in the wilderness.

Even with trucks rumbling down the nearby highway and a jet passing over the valley on its way to L.A., Kyle sometimes felt that he *was* in the wilderness – of the soul, perhaps. Though he had walked through this world for twenty-four years and found it filled with wonders that he knew were God's, he had never had a real message from the Lord.

He had thought of saying this to Corbett during their weekly Pastoral Encounter, but instead he said, "Sometimes it's kind of hard to drive up into people's yards and launch into talk about the Lord. People clam up."

Corbett shrugged, but Kyle persisted. "Some of those people – sometimes I don't think it's worth Your Friend's time."

"No way on earth you, or I, or any man can love people we plain don't like," Corbett said. "And you know what?" He patted Kyle's cheek.

"That's not our job anyway. Our job is to love God. Leave loving the sinner to Him. Besides, the Lord has provided some techniques for our use."

So Kyle learned to prescreen. He scanned the newspapers for signs of trouble – arrest, death, someone's car being broken into – and jotted down the names and addresses of the sufferers. Then he showed up on their doorsteps as if by chance. It was surprising what an effective approach this was. People were eager to share their personal pain.

Ruth Wing had just come in from her studio when she heard someone on the front porch, and she opened the front door as Kyle was about to knock.

"Mrs. Wing? Kyle Bodine," he said. "Outreach Pastor, Your Friend In the Vale." His face went solemn. "Mrs. Wing, I heard about your recent loss, and I wondered if I might be of any use to you."

Ruth looked at him thoughtfully. "Well, I'm an atheist," she said.

"I don't imagine that's much consolation at a time like this."

"I suppose not," she said. She led Kyle into the kitchen. "Excuse my appearance," she said as she washed her hands. "I've been painting all morning." She started the coffeemaker, leaning against the sink as the coffee dripped into the pot.

"Had your husband had been ill, Mrs. Wing?"

"Bum ticker," she said. She had been working on a new niptych, and the dried paint had begun to itch. She folded her arms across her chest, trying to scratch imperceptibly. "I suppose religion does make death easier. It would be nice if I thought Cap was sitting around on his own planet, like a Mormon. Or on a Persian carpet, with naked women dancing around offering him olives."

"A sudden death," Kyle said. "It leaves a lot of unfinished business."

Ruth did not tell this boy that she found she was already forgetting Cap. The day he died she had been feeling irritated at him about something, a familiar, inconsequential irritation at one or more of his annoying habits, but when he died all memory of how irritating he could be was instantly wiped from her brain. And she couldn't remember his eyes. She couldn't remember him ever looking at her.

"Was your husband an atheist, too?"

"Caspar Wing was a Roman Catholic all his life," Ruth said. "But over the years his faith seemed to erode."

"Mrs. Wing," Kyle said, leaning forward a little, "we all have doubts."

A door slammed, and footsteps thudded through the front hall and up the stairs. "My son is staying with me for a while," Ruth said. "He's taken it fairly hard."

Kyle cleared his throat. "Do you think it would help if I talked with him?"

"He's just grieving, really." A few flakes of paint fell out of her sweatshirt as she handed him his coffee.

"Thank you," Kyle said. He stirred in a large spoonful of Cremora. "Well, we all grieve in our own ways."

"Yes," Ruth said, "I'm sure we do."

"Is that one of your paintings?" Kyle was looking at *Nipple Painting #3: Untittled*, which hung above the refrigerator. "I don't know much about art, but it must be a comfort to you."

"Well, I do immerse myself in it," she said.

Footsteps sounded across the ceiling and then down the stairs, and Guy Wing came into the kitchen.

Kyle stood, pushing his chair away from the table. "Kyle Bodine, Outreach Pastor, Your Friend In the Vale. I heard about your loss, Mr. Wing. My condolences."

"Ah," Guy said, shaking Kyle's hand. "Thanks."

"We've just been wondering what Daddy's doing now," Ruth said. "Kyle doesn't think houris are feeding him grapes."

Kyle shook his head. "I admit, I have a fairly traditional Christian view of heaven."

"Let me ask you something," Guy said. He sat down, gripping the edge of the table, and leaned toward Kyle. "Does your setup believe in the Second Coming?" When Kyle nodded, he said, "When do you think it'll be?"

"Well, no on knows the ways of the Lord," Kyle said, "but a lot of people think this is as good a time as any."

Guy reached over and lifted a page on the wall calendar, revealing a grinning golden retriever in a child's party hat. "So if He came back now, how would people know it was really Him?"

"By His works shall ye know Him," Ruth said. Kyle looked at her in surprise.

"But people are always deceiving themselves," Guy said. "They see the Virgin Mary on tortillas, for Chrissake."

Kyle felt sweat on his upper lip. "Well, that's why we study the Bible. The more you understand of the Lord and His ways, the better prepared you are to recognize Him when He comes."

Guy tilted his head. "So you'd know Jesus if you ran into him."

"Yes," Kyle said firmly. "Faith. That's the bottom line, Guy. So many have been misled by the false hope that science and logic and, you know, humanism will lead to understanding. But really, it's only when you have faith that you even begin to understand."

Guy shook his head. "I guess it's beyond me."

Kyle dared to reach over and touch Guy's arm. "That's the first step, recognizing that." He looked at his watch. "Mrs. Wing, I'd like to see more of your artwork sometime."

"Ah," Ruth said. "Do come again."

Kyle turned to Guy. "Talking to a stranger can help when you're dealing with grief. I'd be happy to sit down with you any time."

"Oh," Guy said. "Well, thanks."

They watched from the porch as Kyle crossed the yard and got into his car. At the bottom of the drive he rolled down his window and called, with a little wave, "Condolences!"

They waved back.

"Those guys can smell death from miles away," Guy said as they went inside.

But Ruth felt strangely cheered by the young pastor's visit. He *was* young, too – young enough, almost, to be her grandson, the son of her son.

"The son of my son," she said aloud as she stepped into the shower, and was surprised by an old, almost forgotten sorrow. Well, it was just as well not to have grandchildren. It was hard for children these days. Suppose Guy *had* reproduced, and the child had grown up to be a Christian? It was all very well to continue loving a child who turned out to be not very smart, or a homosexual, but what if it grew up to be a sex offender, or a drug kingpin, or an outreach pastor at a rock 'n' roll church?

Kyle, though, seemed like a nice person. Non-judgmental, as far as she could tell, but of course these people all had their agendas. No one ever accused them of being stupid. His belt was probably hung with the scalps of grieving widows.

She smiled as she remembered him leaning toward her to confide, "We all have doubts."

It was only months after the incident, when John Wayne Turner was going over data with Barron Birdwater, his graduate student, who had finished out the hibernation season alone, that he discovered an actual person had walked him down the hill.

Barron had stayed in camp that morning and – as he reported with some embarrassment – was having an argument with his girlfriend by cellular phone when John Wayne stumbled out of the trees in the arms of a pony-tailed man. Barron had cried "Oh, my God!" and heaved the phone into the air, leaving the girlfriend in the far-away town frightened out of her wits for the rest of the day. Luckily, when Barron regained his own wits, the stranger was able to point out the dense shrubby area where the phone had landed.

Thanks to the global positioning unit that John Wayne had written into his last grant (and to the stranger, who apparently lived in the area), Barron was able to tell the emergency squad exactly where in the rugged mountains of southwestern Oregon John Wayne now lay in shock. Barron then covered John Wayne with sleeping bags, and the two men sat beside him, numb with fear that he would die, until the helicopter came up over the ridge and set down.

"Who was he?" John Wayne said.

"Some old hippy," Barron said. "At first I thought he was holding you hostage."

"He saved my life. Did you get his name?"

"It wasn't exactly my top priority at the time," Barron said. "Anyway, John Wayne, I would've found you. I was on my way to look for you when you showed up."

"Well, I certainly am grateful." John Wayne picked up the graph of heart rate, body temperature, and CO_2 concentration data that Barron had brought in and gazed at it with his one eye. "Looks like you did good work."

It was then Barron cleared his throat and said he had decided to leave the program. In fact, he said, he would be starting nursing school in the fall. When John Wayne stared speechlessly at him, Barron blushed. "It was you, really, that did it. Coming into camp hurt. All I could do was sit there." He looked at his lap and then up again. "You changed my life."

"Well, a lot has changed for everyone." John Wayne said. When the bear's claws scooped out the soft tissues in his eye socket, pierced his sinuses, punctured a eustachian tube, and dragged away a large patch of his cheek, it was *shock* – a physiological reaction – that had started an adrenaline surge, providing his brain with an emergency strategy that kept him moving toward the spot where a man happened to be standing in the woods.

"Biology," he told Barron Birdwater, "is a wonderful thing."

"God's *eye* is on the sparrow." Corbett walked slowly to the very front edge of the stage. "*And* on the sparrow hawk." He stared around the congregation. "What does this tell us about our own sins? And about the sins of others? Our fathers. Our churches. Our government. We can hide nothing from Him. But." Here his back straightened, and he whispered into the mike, *"Neither. Can. They.* Oh, people! Brothers and sisters, we have nothing to fear, because *our* Lord has seen it all!"

He laughed, and the congregation laughed with him, then stood to cheer and applaud and stomp their feet. Eddy up in the booth flipped the red filter over the spotlight, bathing Corbett in a fiery glow. The band started to play as Tyrone Love came out and put an arm across Corbett's shoulders, guiding him backstage to the dressing room.

When Corbett emerged, having showered and changed, Kyle was waiting for him. "Can I ask you something?"

Corbett took a long drink of Pepsi and wiped his mouth with his sleeve. "Of course."

"Do you truly believe the Lord will come in our lifetimes?"

Corbett put down the can and leaned over to put his hand on Kyle's arm. "Listen," he said in a low voice, gazing steadily into Kyle's eyes. "We think He walks among us now."

Kyle saw a tiny featureless Kyle huddled inside each of Corbett's huge pupils. He could almost smell the singed flannel of his shirt and hear his flesh sizzle where Corbett touched him. He shivered. "Here?"

"If not here, where?" Corbett slid both arms around Kyle and pulled him close against his shoulder, patting the back of his neck as if he were a baby. "Trust in the Lord," he said softly. "Be careful what questions you ask. The devil is always on the lookout for advocates."

Kyle drove up into the foothills to a wide spot in the road above the place where the river separated and went around a little island. He made a U-turn in the gravel and parked. It was cool, and though the rain hadn't started to pour yet, the air had dampened.

We think He walks among us now. Could he, Kyle, have seen Him? In some steamy singlewide up in the hills, was that the Lord sitting in a greasy recliner with a hairless little dog on his lap? Or was He a migrant worker, passing through the valley in an old Chevy? A logger? A new recruit hitch-hiking out to the World Of Love Institute?

Or was He right there at Your Friend In the Vale? In the light booth, out in the kitchen, waving cars into the parking lot? Or – and this was the possibility that dried up the inside of Kyle's mouth – up on the stage, preaching to the multitudes?

"No way," Kyle said aloud. There was no way the Lord would lean over and hiss mysteriously into his Outreach Pastor's ear, *We think He walks among us now*. The Lord would not be coy. He would say something like, *Knoweth ye not Who I Am, that ye might Praise Me and be blest?*

He sat looking at the ribbon of damp road stretching down the hill before him. Then he took out his daybook and opened it to the page where he had written *Wing, Guy, abnormal grieving process? Atheist.*

It wasn't often that professed atheists engaged in discussion of the Lord, but Guy Wing had really been interested. He had had a lot of questions. His mother had even quoted Scripture. Of course, anyone can quote scripture if it serves his purpose. Yet Kyle hadn't felt that he was being teased, or deceived. He had felt – well, he had felt something like love, emanating from both the son and the mother. He knew he was confused, but about what, he could not understand.   "I will lift up mine eyes unto the hills, from whence cometh my help," he thought.

He did, and out of the woods on the hill above him stepped a small, thin man. He stood at the edge of the road and slowly turned until he was looking directly down at Kyle. The man – if man he was – was horribly disfigured. He had only half a face.

In that instant Kyle knew with an absolute certainty this was the confrontation he had feared and expected all his Christian life. He was alone in the wilderness, face to face with Satan.

A great roaring was in his ears, and his lungs had ceased to function, so that he could neither expel the acrid, choking air that filled them nor suck in fresh oxygen. In fact the only part of his body that could move was his bowels, which had leaped with alarming vigor into hot, churning action. Kyle felt tears in his eyes. His remains, if there were any, would be found defiled and stinking.

The creature started toward his car.

"Oh, God," Kyle whispered, "I don't have the strength."

But a voice somewhere behind his right ear whispered *Of course you do*. Light flooded through him. If Satan was here in all his manifestations, why, Jesus *must* have returned to walk the earth, and was beside him now!

He bravely rolled down his window and raised his hand. The creature stood still. "I denounce you," Kyle called, "in the name of Jesus."

"Me?" said the creature.

"In the name of Jesus," Kyle said, "get you gone!"

"Wait a minute," the creature said, and as it spoke Kyle saw the darkness in the gaping mouth.

"You have no dominion over me!" Kyle shouted. With a shaking hand he turned the key in the ignition. The car plunged down the hill. When he looked in the rearview mirror, he was not surprised that all he could see in the road behind him was a cloud of dust.

Guy came in from washing the dust off his car, opened the refrigerator door, and stood with the cold air on his face, his eyes closed.

Ruth, entering the kitchen, saw him silhouetted against the light from the open refrigerator, and for the briefest of instants she thought it was Cap, returned in time for dinner from wherever he had gone. In the same synaptic spurt, though, she knew it was not Cap and never would be.

Even so, when Guy turned, a bitter disappointment slid over her shoulders and into a

knot in her throat. She sat at the table. "I thought
for a minute you were your father," she said.

"Dad's ghost, come back for a beer?"

"Your father's ghost would not stand there
letting the cold air out of the refrigerator." Guy put
his beer in her outstretched hand and got another
for himself, closing the door. "Guy, I don't want to
pry, but shouldn't you be getting back to work one
of these days?"

He sat facing her across the table and said
glumly, "No one buys cars this time of year,
Mom." He watched her trace a pattern in the
condensation on her bottle. "If I tell you something,
will you not laugh?"

"I'll give it a try," Ruth said.

So he told her about waking up as Jesus
Christ. "I don't know what to do. I mean, I still feel
as if it could be true."

His mother took a long swallow of beer.
"This sort of thing happened to your father now
and then."

"You're kidding!" Guy said. "Dad thought
he was Jesus Christ?"

"No, he thought he had brain cancer. He
said good-bye to everyone and wrote out a new
will. Then he sat in the living room waiting for
death. When it didn't come by the end of the week
he went back to work as if nothing had happened."

"Oh," Guy said. It didn't sound like the
same sort of thing.

Ruth looked out the window at the late
afternoon sun shining on the hills across the valley.
"Another time he woke up thinking he could
communicate with horses. He was all set to go to
Nevada and walk among herds of wild mustangs."

"What happened?"

She frowned. "I don't remember. Something kept him from going, and then he just forgot about it, I guess. At least, he stopped talking about it."

Guy too stared out the window, seeing not the view of the mountains that his mother had painted a thousand times before she switched to nipple art but his father, in faded jeans and a checkered shirt, walking out among the lethal flying hooves into the middle of a dusty corral. He raised his hands, palms up, and the angry, snorting, foaming beasts stopped their rampage. Nostrils flaring, eyes rolling, lips curled back to display their huge yellow teeth, they edged closer and closer to Caspar Wing, a man who, to his son's knowledge, had never been any closer to a horse than he'd been to a stegosaurus, and began to whicker, and bumped his hands with their soft noses, and lowered their big heads so he could scratch behind their ears.

"Do you think Dad was happy?" he said.

"People with big imaginations are rarely happy."

"You've always seemed happy."

"Well, Guy, whatever creative impulse I have isn't the imaginative type. When you can't imagine frightening or bad things, they don't bother you."

Guy looked doubtfully at his mother. *Your mother is delicate*, Cap used to say. *An artiste. She sees things we don't.* It was his pragmatic father who paid the bills, fixed the leaks, started the fire in the stove in the morning.

But maybe it had been the other way around all along. Maybe Ruth was the practical one, firmly setting her visions on canvas where they could be seen and understood, and Cap was the one who saw what wasn't there.

And now Guy was having the wildest visions of all. Dreaming of being Jesus Christ, for God's sake! Worse, telling himself that selling cars was the way he wanted to live his life. Now *there* was a terrific imagination. Because when he told his mother that he liked selling cars he was not exactly lying, but he was stretching the truth.

He did love BMW's, the bulk and sleekness of them, the cold sturdiness of their bumpers under the palm of his hand. He was a good salesman and proud of it. But selling cars was not the way he had expected to close out his youth. No matter how good he was at it – how large his commissions were, how fast he could close a deal – ultimately, he considered himself a failure. But you couldn't tell your old mother, who thought you were God's gift to the world, that you were a failure.

"It would have been nice to be able to say good-bye," he said.

"A sudden death leaves a lot of unfinished business." Ruth drained her beer and stood up. "Guy, if you want to spend your old age as Jesus, that's your privilege. I'm going to spend mine painting."

"Pastor Hildebrand, I've seen Satan," Kyle said as Corbett entered the office.

Corbett closed the door behind him. "Where was this, Brother Kyle?"

"Up in the woods," Kyle said. "I was praying in my car, and I looked up and there he was. Like he was expecting me."

"What did he look like?" Corbett asked.

Kyle saw again the gaping mouth, the darkness where there should have been a face. "Pure evil. The demon walked in a cloud of darkness, and from his mouth poured filth and abomination. He started for me, but I told him I'd have no truck with him. To get him gone."

"What did he do?" Corbett had crossed the room to stand behind his desk, his fingertips just touching the desktop.

"Sissed at me. I drove away, and when I looked back he was gone in a puff of smoke." It could have been smoke, he thought; maybe dust, maybe smoke.

"Brother Kyle," Corbett said, "how do you know it was Satan?"

"I've prayed about it," Kyle said. "I think it's a sign from the Lord. I think He wanted me to see how desperate Satan is. I believe Satan has showed himself to me because the Lord Jesus Christ is walking ever closer to me."

Corbett came around the desk. "I've known this was coming. I've seen it coming to you," he said softly. "They're in battle over your immortal soul. You have a long road ahead of you." He took Kyle's hands. "I want you to pray with me now."

They got down on their knees on the carpet.

"Brother Kyle," Corbett said, "the Lord has asked me to help you on your way."

Kyle lifted his head. "It's a road we'll take together, then?"

"Brother Kyle," Corbett said, "I am with you every step of the way."

Ruth sat on the sofa staring at the skylight, which had a thick grey spider web in one corner

and a collection of dead leaves along the bottom.
She wondered if she'd laid it on a bit thick with
Guy. She had always thought Cap's obsessions
were more a sign of pathology than of an active
imagination. But you couldn't say to your son,
Daddy was a crackpot, dear. If Guy hadn't noticed
that when his father was alive, there was no point
in bringing it up now.

She didn't think Cap had much
imagination. Her nipple technique had embarrassed
him. "The nipple is not a *tool*," he had grumbled;
and when she pointed out that men have certain
tools while women have others, his forehead had
gone red, and he had asked what she was planning
to fix for lunch.

She had *liked* the idea of the nipple as tool.
It was the perfect implement, providing both
nourishment and delight, the gateway not only to
life but to its very source. By immersing her
nipples in paint she immersed herself in the process
of creation; which is, she thought now, a way of
connecting with what is called the divine.

At the sound of a car in the driveway she
went to the door. A pickup had stopped at the foot
of the steps, and as the driver got out she gasped,
then laughed at herself. It was a trick of the light.
What at first glance looked like a chunk of missing
face was really an oversized black patch, like a
pirate's, held on by an elastic band; below it a
smooth sheet of bright scar tissue glistened like
liquid in the sunlight. It was as if a Picasso had
come to life at her front door.

"I'm looking for a man named Guy Wing,"
the man said.

"Well, you've found his mother."

He came up the steps and took her hand in

both of his. "Your son saved my life. It took me a long time to find out his name."

"I'm afraid you just missed him," Ruth said. "He's gone back to the dealership."

Guy sped toward Beaverton, a liter of beer tucked between his thighs. *Your old age* his mother had said, and at her words he had seen himself forgotten, divorced, childless, having failed his father, doomed to watch the end of the world as he had known it, unreprieved by the promised birth of the new. The vision had first depressed him and then, slowly, it had filled him with pleasure.

There was his answer: *Jesus as an old fart!* He would live the *second* half of Jesus's life, the part that had never been done. He could solicit disciples and lecture them; he could get someone to design a Web page for him and deliver the truth over the Internet. Or he could sell BMW's in Beaverton, and drink beer, and dispense good works as the need arose. Pure poetry.

He took a drink, resettled the bottle between his legs, and reached for the cruise control.

I'LL MEET YOU THERE

He drives, she navigates. Everything is dry and bright. There are many, many cars, there is a long highway, there are billboards and there are low flat houses clustered together with nothing between them and the sun but flat red roofs. Each house sits in a gravel yard, adorned here and there with an artistic grouping of large rocks and a few cacti.

"I can't wait any longer." Williams turns off the highway onto a gravel road that runs past one of these little housing developments and pulls over beside a scramble of bushes and broken glass. When he opens the car door and springs out the heat pours in around him. Marian listens to his pee sizzle as it hits the ground.

"Marian, could you get me my camera?" Within seconds of stepping into the desert Williams has found a rattlesnake. "I knew I shouldn't have put it in the trunk."

She gets out of the car, looking carefully at the ground before she puts her feet down, and walks around to the trunk, sure that at any moment something will squirm under her feet, and she opens the trunk and shoves the suitcase around so she can reach the zipper. She pulls out the camera case and takes the camera out of it and then walks on as little of the surface of her feet as she can over to where Williams is grinning at the snake.

"Here," she says.

She doesn't hurry back to the car, though. She stands in the heat and looks out at the landscape, which is ugly. The yards are coated with blinding green grass and the unimproved ground surrounding the development is brown, dusty dirt. Above them the sky is an unlikely blue and there are no clouds. She is ready to turn around and drive back to the airport and take the next plane to a cooler, duller state when, ten feet in front of her, a roadrunner rushes from one side of the road to the other.

"Beepbeep!" Marian cries, without even thinking.

When the phone rang, Hank was working in the kitchen. He put down his drill. "Go ahead, answer it," he said. "It might be the voice of Fate."

"Marian," the voice on the other end said, "I'm getting married."

"That's wonderful," Marian said. "Louise?"

"Who did you think it was?" Louise said. "Look, I want you to give me away."

"What?" Marian said.

"You're my last living connection to Daddy. It would say so much if you could stand in for him."

"Couldn't I just represent him in the audience?" Marian said.

"Come on, Mar," Louise said.

"What does your mother say?" Marian said.

"I don't care what she says," Louise said.

"It's *my* wedding."

"I'm not sure I could handle it, Louise."

"Of course you could," Hank said.

"Is someone there with you?" Louise said. "Your dark young friend?"

"It's Hank from across the street," Marian said. "You met him during the trial."

"No I didn't," Louise said. "You didn't introduce me to anyone."

"Surely I did," Marian said.

"Don't be defensive, Marian," Louise said. "It really doesn't matter. Anyway. Will you come?"

"I suppose so," Marian said.

"That's great," Louise said. "Wear anything you want. It's very informal. Bring your little friend."

"I haven't even talked to her in *years*," Marian said to Hank when she hung up. "Why on earth would she want me to give her away?"

"Maybe she loves you," Hank said.

"Maybe she just wants to bug her mother."

"Oh, come on," Hank said. "She's how old?"

"In her eighties somewhere," Marian said.

"I mean your stepdaughter," Hank said. "Isn't she a little old to be fighting with her mother?"

"You're never too old to fight with your mother," Marian said. She closed her eyes and saw herself striding down an aisle, hauling Louise by the wrist, Louise struggling to keep up. It *is* a sort of nice thing, she thought; a way to include Arthur on this day. Though surely the presence of Louise's mother – and the presence of Louise herself – would *imply* Arthur. Well, it would be interesting to see Louise again, after all this time. And what sort of man she was marrying.

"Sounds like a blast," Hank said.

"Come on, baby, come on." Williams is
down on his belly in front of the rattlesnake,
camera in one hand, a yellow stalk of dead grass in
the other, pointing it toward the snake's nose.
"Let's see some fang, babe."

Marian supposes in an emergency she
could run to the nearest of the low white houses,
though no sign of life is visible in any of them. A
Mexican maid would probably answer the door.
She imagines herself saying "Snake!" very loudly,
enunciating clearly. "Rattle!" Shaking an imaginary
baby rattle and then, at the woman's
uncomprehending look, putting her palms together
and waving her arms around, weaving her hips,
trying to look serpentine. In college a girl named
Beth had told her she had just the right figure for
belly dancing: *wide in the hips, thin and snaky on
top*.

The maid would turn out to be the missus
and would call back over her shoulder, into the
dark cool depths of the tiled hall, "Harry! Another
tourist got bit."

From the darkness a man's belly would
emerge, followed by the man himself in a
sleeveless undershirt, a soggy cigar hanging from
his lip, his grizzled hair in a brush cut and his
spectacles thicker than oil. "Where y'all from?"
he'd gargle, and Marian would notice plastic tubes
running from his nostrils to a tank that he pulled
along beside him.

"Saratoga Springs," she'd say. "Please
come." And she'd belly dance her way back
through the housing development, the old fart

gasping behind her, the wife scurrying along behind carrying the oxygen tank, to where Williams lay writhing on the ground, clutching his wrist above the spot where two gaping holes were rapidly disappearing into a bulbous swollen mass of flesh, and the villainous snake had slithered with silent satisfaction into the shade of a greasewood bush.

"Thanks, bud," Williams says. He gets to his knees, then to his feet. The snake is coiled up now, head raised, looking for all the world like a snake.

"Don't you think you're a little old to crawl around on the desert floor?" Marian says. Little bits of gravel and something sparkly like glass are embedded in the flesh of his elbows and knees.

"Never too old to grovel for my art, babe," he says.

Louise is also an artist, in a red-lipsticked, chain-smoking, brassy-haired way. She paints tiny, tiny little pictures, exquisite miniatures, on the heads of matches, the shafts of pine needles, anything so small Marian can see it only if she takes off her bifocals and holds it very close to her face.

"What's the point?" she asked Arthur once.

"Art needs no point," he'd explained in a voice that sounded very, very kind, but in fact was designed to make the interlocutor feel very, very stupid. He was tremendously defensive where His Girl was concerned

And in fact Louise has achieved a certain degree of fame in what Marian believes is the art world. Once she and Arthur went to one of Louise's shows, where her works were displayed

135

beneath magnifying glasses. People strolled from glass to glass, leaning over and producing positive-sounding murmurs. Once in a while they cried out and leaned closer to peer in.

"Are you sure this is the right road?" They have turned off the highway onto a secondary road, then onto a tertiary road, a track which is unpaved and so small it isn't even on the map Marian holds.

"Sure. I've been through here before." Williams has traveled around the area a number of times, though he has never stayed at The Back of Beyond, the inn where Louise will be getting married tomorrow.

"Why do you suppose Louise is having her wedding in the middle of nowhere?" Marian says.

"Lots of people get married there. You'll probably want to too, once you see it."

"I don't think so," Marian says. She likes the desert okay, but in small doses and for very short periods of time. She thinks Man in the Desert is like Man on the Moon, or Man On a Crowded Subway: All the preparation in the world is terrific as long as there is no accident. That For Which One Cannot Prepare.

They bump along. The vegetation has changed: there are tall yellow grasses and some yucca variants that are either just past or just about to bloom. Now and then they come to a wide flat puddle in the middle of the road. At the first one Williams stops, gets out of the car, and inches his way out into the middle of the water, where he looks right and left before coming back.

"What were you looking for?" Marian says.

"Flash floods," he says.

136

"In the desert?" She wonders if he's gotten too much sun.

"Absolutely," he says, driving the car very slowly through the puddle. "A wall of water can come on you so fast you don't know what hit you. *Never* step into one of those arroyos if there's even a *hint* of clouds."

"That was an arroyo?" Marian has begun to worry just a little about reaching the Back of Beyond in time for the wedding rehearsal, which is at four o'clock. She can't imagine why they are going this way. It isn't as if a sign had said *Scenic Viewpoint* or *Point of Interest*. There is no reason to be driving up this dirt road at midday under a killer sun.

When they come upon the stalled van she immediately gets a bad feeling. Even under its coating of yellow dust it's too bright to look at. Williams slows the little car and is just easing to the left to drive around the van when a man who has been underneath it scrambles to his feet, semaphoring his arms over his head to get their attention. His naked belly is streaked with grease and glistening with sweat. Williams stops the car.

"Don't get out," Marian whispers.

The man jogs around to Williams's side of the car and leans down. "Man am I glad to see you," he says, talking so fast Marian can hardly understand him. "Could you give me a jump? Because I can't get the engine started, could be the starter but there are other possibilities and I can't eliminate them. Can you jump me?"

"I don't have any cables," Williams says.

"I've got them, if you could pull your car up I can do all the work, I'm a mechanic but if you

could just let me try them on your engine I think I
could get it started. That's all it needs." The man
wears no hat and no sunglasses, and the whites of
his small, red-rimmed eyes stand out in his dark
face. He doesn't look at Williams, but glances right
and left, back and forth, as he speaks. Sweat
streams down on either side of his nose into the
gullies carved past his mouth, and drops of it fall
from his chin.

"Sure," Williams says.

The man throws his hands up in an
awkward gesture, of relief or perhaps victory, and
jogs around the car to the back of his van. Fat
joggles above the waistband of his slick green
pants.

"I don't like this," Marian says in a low
voice.

Williams shakes his head. "This is the
desert, Mar. People can die."

The man is rummaging around in the dim
interior of his van. When Marian lowers her
sunglasses she can see inside; it's stuffed with
boxes and piles of fabric and wadded newspapers
and bottles and beat-up boots and coils of rope. A
jar half-filled with black liquid stands on the
ground beside the right rear tire. The man
straightens up, waving the jumper cables. Williams
backs and saws the car until it is nose to nose with
the van, and reaches down to pop the hood.

"Jesus, Williams, that's the trunk." That's
the last thing they need, to display their personal
belongings to this guy. She opens her door and
climbs out and the heat drops on her like a
collapsing tent. She struggles through it to slam the
trunk closed.

The man fixes the cables on the contact

points and clambers into the driver's seat of the
van, and Williams revs the engine. Marian trudges
a little way up a rise beside the road, feeling as if
she is barely moving. There are yellow sunflowery
things blooming among the grey bunch grasses, and
in the distance she can see a hint of mountains,
faint and blurred at the end of the endless desert.
The man is shouting at Williams through the noise
of the engine and Williams is nodding as he sits in
the car, his foot on the gas.

Marian wonders if she will know when
they are about to die. The guy is probably a
veteran, off drugs for now but way, way down on
his luck, and nuts. He's probably done this before,
pretending to have trouble with his van and then
when his Samaritans' defenses are down he kills
them. Buries them in the desert, takes their water,
and drives merrily away. The little rented car will
be found but this clever guy will be long gone. No
one will ever know what happened.

Marian and Williams will disappear
without a trace.

Williams revs the engine when the man
waves his hand, lets it slow when the man motions
downward.

How do people get through life, she
wonders. How on earth do you get through life
with no money and no intelligence and no luck?

The van doesn't start. Marian sits on a rock
watching the man run back and forth from the
engine to the back of the van, hauling grease-
blackened tools from soggy cardboard boxes. She
winces as he drops to the ground and pushes
himself under the car, no little wheeled dolly, not
even a piece of cardboard between his flesh and the

dirty gravel. He *must* be on drugs, she thinks, that
he doesn't feel the gravel digging into his bare
back.

Williams gets out of the car and goes over
to look into the engine. "I don't think it's the
battery," she hears him say. The guy must have
said something from under the car because
Williams says, "No, more like the alternator," at
which the man's arms drop to the ground at his
sides as if in defeat. He lies still for a moment, then
digs his heels into the ground and drags himself
out.

Holding a wrench, he gets up and walks
over to stand beside Williams.

Move away from him, Marian thinks, her
heart speeding. *Just slowly step away*.

Williams, having no instinct for self-
preservation, doesn't respond. Instead he leans
forward and points at something under the hood.
The man looks at the back of Williams's head for a
long moment before he too leans forward to look.

Marian stands up and looks around again,
but no car has appeared on the snake of road that
lies like a mirage across the gray-green desert.
Suppose the man does something to Williams. Or
suppose Williams just keels over in the heat. They
have one small bottle of water in the car which by
now is probably hot enough to make tea. She
would bathe Williams's face and wet his lips and
drag him into the shade of the car; then what?
Leave him with the man while she goes for help?
Send the man for help? Sit companionably with the
crazy man and wait to be found?

She would break off the rearview mirror
and use it to flash signals at passing jets. She would
break the mirror itself and flash it at the man if he

should threaten her or Williams.

Williams walks over and reaches into the back seat of the car and brings out his camera bag. He takes the camera out of the case and fiddles with it, then walks back to where the man is still leaning into the engine. Williams says something and the man jerks his head up. Williams raises his hand as if to say *stay* and the man stays motionless. Williams steps back and raises the camera, and Marian sees the man's bright teeth. Williams leans over the engine and takes its picture, then walks around and takes a picture of the back of the van and the innards littering the ground.

He's a genius, Marian thinks. *Not an artist, but a genius.* She stands up and walks slowly back to the car.

"Anything," the man is saying. He doesn't look at her, but he doesn't look at Williams either, who stands with his arms folded against his chest and his camera in one hand as he listens to the man. The man looks at his own empty hand, at the right front tire of the rental car, at the hood of the van, propped open above the engine. "Give me enough time and the right tools and I can repair anything. I'm a skilled worker. You've heard of those Indians, those Mohawks, that do that highwire construction work, balancing on the edge of heights? I can do that with any kind of mechanical piece. If I have the right tools, you know? But the water here is polluted, chromium, toluene, you name it. Look at it." He gestures toward the jar of black water. "No way I would put that in my engine, you know?"

"Is that all the water you have?" Williams says. "You can't stay out here without water."

"A decent wrench would make the

difference," the man says.

"Not without water," Williams says. "Look, I've been out here before. No one might come this way for weeks."

"We've got some," Marian says. She reaches into the back seat and pulls out the bottle of water she would have used to bathe Williams's fevered brow. It *is* warm. She holds it out to the man, who takes it without looking at her. "We could leave this with you. We don't need it."

Williams looks at her. "You know how long that would last, babe?"

"It's all we've *got*, Williams," she says.

Williams turns back to the man and says, "We'll take you into town."

"It could be I need a new alternator," he says. "It's been known to happen. If I just had the right tools I could get it running good enough to get me to town. Even a wrench."

"Look, lock up your van and we'll take you into town. You can load up on water and get what you need."

"I could get the wrench," the man says hopelessly, and he heads for the back of the van.

"Williams, we have to be there by four o'clock," Marian says.

"Marian, it's just the rehearsal." She sees him place an extremely patient look on his face. "We can't leave this guy out here."

Of course she knows that. People die in this heat, dozens of them every year. She's seen it in the papers; she's tried to imagine the desperation that drives people to leave what homes they know and cross the desert. When all that waits for even the luckiest is janitorial work and a hot apartment shared by twenty people.

Saving illegal Mexicans is one thing, but a serial killer?

The smell of the man's body oozes up and surrounds her, and with each bump and pothole the sharp, aggressive odor of his breath surges forward and curls around her head, right at nose level. She holds her sun hat over her nose and mouth. He talks nonstop for the two hours and eighteen minutes it takes to drive to Tucson, but he doesn't give them any information about himself, he doesn't ask anything about them, and he barely responds when Williams responds to him. After he ignores several of her remarks, Marian stops trying to be kind. The man is clearly disturbed, and there's no point in trying to pretend he isn't. They'll be lucky to get to Tucson alive.

But they do, and they spend another hour driving through the ugly flat traffic-ridden streets of Tucson's low-rent outskirts looking for Road Runner Auto Repair. By the time they find it, it has closed for the day, although it is only three o'clock. They stand helplessly before the crude but recognizable roadrunner hand-painted on the shop's glass door, the words *BeepBeep!* rising from its mouth in a little white balloon. Williams points out that lots of repair shops close early in the day, since they often start at godawful hours in the morning, and besides, it's Friday.

"And?" Marian says. She has the sudden feeling that Williams and the man are in cahoots. She has been with them all afternoon, all day, and they have never said anything that indicated any kind of conspiracy, but she feels that somehow they have made a secret agreement without her knowledge, as if men can communicate with grunts and gestures and odors that a woman knows nothing of.

But then the man says, "My sister." He throws his arm down, as if he were hurling a heavy tool to the ground. "I'm calling her!" he shouts, and he stomps over to yank the car door open. He leans in and takes something from the depths of the greasy bag he brought with him. They hear a series of tiny *beeps*.

Williams and Marian look at each other.

"A cell phone," she says.

Williams's face is lined and gray under the russet flush from the day's overdose of sunlight, and the whites of his eyes are red. He isn't as young as he used to be, and now he has spent all day trying to help a man in trouble. In *danger*. Marian is embarrassed at the thought of her grumpiness. She rolls her eyes and then smiles at him, hoping he understands she's mocking the troubled man and making light of the fact that they are about to miss the wedding rehearsal and in another hour they will start missing the rehearsal dinner.

"She's coming to get me." The man shouts as if they are a block away. As he comes toward them Marian notices that he walks unsteadily. An inner ear problem, maybe. "She said, 'Oh, you're at the Road Runner, I'm on my way.' She doesn't want to know about me, but she does."

"Yeah, my family's like that," Williams says. "They don't want to know about me, either, but they can't help it."

"You can go now," the man says, waving the cell phone. "My sister's coming so you can go now."

"We can wait," Williams says pleasantly.

"No, no, no, you go," the man says. "I'm waiting for her." He looks over his shoulder, then moves sideways until he reaches the shop door, and he leans back on it so that for a moment the *BeepBeep!* balloon is rising right out of his head. Then he slides down and sits against the door with his knees drawn up, clutching the greasy bag and the cell phone to his chest. "I'm waiting," he says loudly.

"Really, it's no trouble," Marian says, but the man turns his face away.

"We'll wait till she comes," Williams says firmly.

The man closes his eyes and shakes his head. "No, no no no no." His voice rises with each *no*. "My sister's coming. You go *now*."

And so they drive off, leaving the man sitting in front of the Road Runner. Marian waves, but he doesn't wave back.

"Do you think he really has a sister?" she says.

"Well." Williams sighs. "I don't think he's capable of making her up."

The sun is still strong, but it's so low in the sky that the shadows of the buildings lie across the street; the car moves through a cool grey square of shade, then a hot patch of blinding light that shoots in at the side of Marian's sunglasses, then back into shadow again. Hot bright / cool gray / hot bright / cool gray.

"Strobe City," she says.

"Why is it always Something City with you?" Williams says.

She looks at him. This side of his face is untouched by the strobing of the sun.

"Why can't you say *The sun is making patterns on my eyes*? Instead you say *Strobe City* and I'm supposed to laugh."

"You're not supposed to laugh," she says. "I just said it. It doesn't mean anything."

"Don't you take anything seriously?"

"I take everything seriously," Marian says. "Ever since Arthur I can hardly even breathe."

"You think you're the only one?" He pulls into the parking lot of an abandoned strip mall and turns off the engine, and sits gripping the steering wheel. "I signed on too, you know. Late, maybe. But I'm here now."

In the middle of a dead and dry planting strip a white plastic shopping bag impaled on a prickly pear cactus is whipping madly in the wind. It whips and whips and gets nowhere.

Marian reaches over and takes Williams's hand. "For a long time I liked to think that I'd find happiness with someone." She closes her eyes. "I could see a big, rolling meadow with a copse of oaks at the far edge, and I could see myself walking out through tall grass and swaying seedheads to meet someone who was in it somewhere. Then I met Arthur, and for a long time I thought it was him."

"You were younger then," Williams says. "How could you even imagine me?"

They watch the dancing bag.

"Maybe we should go back and check on him," Marian says.

"That guy was scary," he says, frowning. "I can't believe we let him in our car."

"Well, what were we supposed to do?"

"Ask if he had a cell phone," Williams says. "Jesus, can you believe it?"

"You're the tech guy," she says. "Maybe you should sign us up for the twenty-first century."

He laughs and holds her hand to his lips. Then he starts up and they drive back to Road Runner Auto Repair.

The man isn't there, though. No sign of him. No sister, no cell phone, no serial killer. There is nothing to do but turn around and go on. They stop for burritos. Then, while Williams gases up, Marian uses an old-fashioned pay phone to call The Back of Beyond.

"The missing stepmother!" cries the woman who answers the phone. "Are you all right, hon?"

Marian says she is. She tells the woman to tell Louise that she'll be there late tonight.

"She'll be tickled to hear it," the woman says. "But I think you're in trouble, sweetheart."

In the dim light of dusk the geography is transformed. As they drive away from the city the land swells up from the highway into little hills and cliffs, and as the road curves around a rise tiny mountains materialize at the horizon, dark against the white-blue sky.

"What mountains are those?" Marian says. She looks over at Williams. He has fallen asleep, his head back against the headrest and his mouth open.

Tomorrow it will seem like such a non-emergency, a non-event! A man's car broke down and Williams and Marian took him back into town and dropped him off at a car repair shop.

"*Now* will you get a cell phone?" Louise will say.

But for tonight they're safe. All the way to

the Back of Beyond Marian thinks of the man's
sweaty, dirty skin and smells the sickening odor of
his breath. She imagines what would have
happened if she and Williams hadn't stopped. She
pictures the man's body, desiccated and stark and
torn, the turkey vultures beadily snacking away.
She sees the old van, bleached and sand-blasted,
standing in the desert forever, all those papers and
tools and greasy rags scattered across the sand.

That American dream, Marian thinks.
People think you can just pack up and go. Just go,
and leave it all behind.

DEUS EX MACHINA

Just before she goes, Sara glances again at the sky. The days this fall have been unusually clear across the west. Nothing stands between Sara and the universe but the worn blanket of atmosphere that makes the sky blue.

Then, as so often happens in life, the phone rings.

It's Ardith, calling from New York. In the past, years have gone by during which Sara and Ardith were not in touch, but lately Ardith calls every few months, just to say hello and in passing to relate more events of her eventful life to her old friend in the west. Ardith was a corporate attorney who left her Boston firm in order to sculpt, and has been so successful that now she travels around the world sculpting on demand, and doing large-scale installations, and teaching master classes in various kinds of sculpting. She travels everywhere in the world except to the Pacific Northwest, about which she has had a vision which involved her own death in a cataclysmic event.

"Oh my god, and I called right at this moment!" Ardith says when Sara tells her she's on the way to a funeral. "Sara, it's reaching out for me."

"Ardith, an old lady fell asleep at the wheel." Sara doesn't bother to point out that for all its earthquakes, volcanoes, and automobile accidents, the Northwest is statistically a hell of a lot safer than Manhattan. She knows that Ardith has transferred her fears from where she lives now to a place she doesn't need to be. "Don't be high-strung. I only have a minute. What's up?"

"The reason I called, besides an irresistible urge, is to tell you I'm getting married."

"Married! Who on earth are you going to marry?"

"You sound shocked," Ardith says, trying to sound offended but unable to hide the pleasure she feels at having astonished her old friend. "And it's *whom*. His name is Ivan, and he's a retired aerospace engineer."

"Ivan," Sara says carefully. "Have you mentioned him before?"

"I may have mentioned his son Sam, the architect on the Chicago project."

"Ah," Sara says. She doesn't remember a Chicago project. "Ardith, I really do have to go. Can I call you later?"

"We're eloping to Paris tonight," Ardith says. "I'll call you when we get back."

Eloping to Paris, eloping to Paris. As Sara drives down the hill she meets Melrita coming up. Melrita pulls over to let her pass. She has started to roll down the window, but Sara smiles and waves and doesn't stop. For most of the last century Melrita's family owned acres and acres of land around here, until Melrita started selling off bits and pieces of it, including the lot and the house where Sara and Jonah live. Not only has Melrita never been to Paris, she's hardly been out of the county.

"To everything there is a season." Jasmine Korn's daughter has flown in from San Diego and is here in the Children's Department, standing in the middle of the bright United States-shaped carpet, surrounded by more than fifty people, most of them with white or little hair, who sit on tiny chairs, gazing up as raptly as if she were reading *Horton Hears A Who*, though of course *Ecclesiastes* can be riveting too. Jasmine, a sweet little old librarian who befriended Sara when she first started working at the library, was killed in an automobile accident on her way home from the casino up at Cow Creek. She was 83 years old.

Eloping to Paris, eloping to Paris. Perched on a bright red chair labeled IN MEMORY OF TAMMY ANN WRIGLEY, Sara pictures Ardith standing at the top of a set of rolling stairs, waving at a crowd. Beside her a tall, white-haired man in an impeccably tailored grey suit has one hand on the small of her back and is waving with the other. They turn and disappear into the body of a Concorde aimed at Paris. A stewardess smiling brilliantly reaches out to pull the door closed behind them, the stairs are rolled away, and the Concorde, a massive black shape with a hundred brightly-lit golden portholes, backs away from the terminal and starts moving toward the runway. *Eloping to Paris.*

After the service there's a reception in the community meeting room. People mill about clutching pale cookies and sipping at the strange red punch that is served at every library function Sara has ever attended. Everyone's chatting and laughing as if they were at the annual Friends of the Library tea. Don, a cataloger, introduces her to the dead woman's daughter, Elaine.

Sara says she's sorry about Jasmine's death.

Elaine frowns. "She went fast and rich. You heard she won over three hundred dollars that day?" She gestures at the bright carpet and chairs and paintings on the wall. "This is nice. Mother slaved so hard for so many years in that dump, and then as soon as she retires they build this."

A shelver approaches to offer Elaine some more condolences and Sara inches away. As she refills her cup with red punch, her supervisor, Alma, the head of the reference department, introduces her to Dana Sheffield, an elegantly dressed library trustee.

"Oh, hello," Sara says. Jonah has mentioned Dana Sheffield, who is also on the board of KindErth. "I'm Sara McDonald, Jonah's wife."

Dana Sheffield frowns. "Jonah?"

"Jonah McDonald," Sara says. "He's executive director for KindErth."

"Yes, I know," Dana says. "You're his ex-wife?"

Sara laughs. "Not that I know of."

"I thought I'd met Jonah's wife," Dana says. "It must have been someone else's wife." She leans forward to touch Sara's arm. "You may have saved me from a very great embarrassment."

Sara will remember this later.

"We need to ask you some questions, ma'am." It's the very next day, the day after Jasmine Korn's memorial service, and Sheriff Floyd Peach and a man Sara doesn't know are standing on her front doorstep.

"Must be serious if you're calling me *ma'am,* Floyd," she says, because she and Floyd have been on a first-name basis ever since he came into the library and she found him a book on découpage a decade or more ago.

"I'm afraid it is," he says, taking off his sunglasses. "May we come in?"

She feels her stupidly smiling cheeks freeze. "What's the matter?" she says. "Is it Jonah?"

"Why do you ask?" the stranger says, looking alertly into her eyes.

"He's her husband, Seth," Floyd says, and he tells Sara, "Yes and no. We need to ask you some questions."

Seth Miller is from the FBI, and by the time he has asked Sara half a dozen questions she has begun to suspect that there is more to Jonah than has met her eye, but she tries not to let on that she suspects this.

"Your bank records and income tax returns are being subpoenaed, so you might as well tell us right now," Seth says. He is dark, with liquid brown eyes and a brown moustache sprinkled with grey that generously drapes his upper lip. He seems very sad, as if all this hurts him far more than it will hurt Sara. "What *is* your income, Mrs. McDonald?"

"I hardly make anything," she says, feeling confused. "Jonah has a trust fund, but it's not very big. I mean, it pays the mortgage. He doesn't make that much. I guess he does pretty well, but I'm not sure how much he gets." She feels deeply humiliated listening to herself babble. *Traditional stupid wife,* she thinks.

"Yes, we know he does pretty well," Seth says solemnly, and then he and Floyd Peach both suddenly grin, bright flashes of teeth in the darkening room that are quickly extinguished. "What's going on?" Sara says. "Has something happened? Should I get a lawyer?" She briefly pictures Ardith, the closest thing to a lawyer that she has, clutching her briefcase in one hand and holding a fashionable hat on her head with the other as she rushes through the rain toward the waiting Concorde, the tall elderly man who must be Ivan hurrying after her with his arms full of shopping bags.

"Now, I may be speaking a little bit out of turn here," Floyd says, glancing at Seth and then back at Sara. "You personally are not the target of this investigation, Sara. But you might do well to contact your lawyer on a more personal matter. The thing is, it looks like Jonah has committed, uh, bigamy."

Sara blats out a laugh. "Hah!" She looks from Floyd to Seth Miller, who nods sadly.

"He left a paper trail as wide as the Oregon Trail," he says. (Sara will someday use the analogy herself.) "We have receipts for suspect personal items and household expenses for a second home. But it's unlikely we'll prosecute on that matter. We're more interested in the evidence that he has embezzled several hundred thousand dollars from KindErth." He looks around the room, then back at Sara. "You don't seem to have many books, Mrs. McDonald."

"Books?" she says.

"There's evidence that Jonah buys a lot of books," Seth says. "But I guess he doesn't keep them here."

A spurt of relief flashes across her shoulders. They've got the wrong guy: *Jonah has never been a purchaser of books!* Both of them have always disliked the idea of amassing shelves full of books, read once and left to collect dust; they're big library users.

But the flash is just a flash; it's the *other* wife who likes to own books.

During the entire visit, despite his grim and threatening speech, Seth Miller has retained the sad look on his face, and by the time he and Floyd stand up to leave Floyd has developed it, too. Both men stand looking at Sara as if they have brought her tidings of great grief, after which the world will never be the same. (The next time she looks in the mirror, that same look will be caught in the 52-year-old lines and creases of her face.)

"Is there someone we can call?" Floyd says. "A friend?"

"No one," Sara says, and to her embarrassment it comes out in a loud half-hysterical sob, at which Seth Miller winces.

"Mrs. McDonald," he says, "you need to be prepared for the media. The press is going to be on this."

She looks at him in horror. "You mean this is going to be publicized?"

"Sara, it's a criminal prosecution," Floyd says.

"I thought you were leaving the – I thought you were only prosecuting the money thing," she says.

"We have to document how we found out," Seth says.

"The Oregon Paper Trail." She giggles, picturing a Conestoga wagon wobbling through the prairie grasses, an ankle-deep swath of receipts and marriage licenses fluttering in its wake.

"Ma'am?" he says, a look of alarm on his face.

He thinks I've lost it, she thinks.

All afternoon Sara stays on the sofa where she sank down after Floyd and Seth Miller left. The sun moves across the sky, and its long light slides listlessly across the floor and then grows thin. Late in the day Charles Catz thumps onto the ledge outside the kitchen, pops through his cat door, and lands with a thud on the floor. She turns her head to look at him and he stands frozen, eyes wide, staring at her, for a number of long, slow seconds, until suddenly his right rear leg shoots straight out at an impossible angle and he leans down to clean his bottom. After another moment he looks at her again and makes a loud, probably rude remark.

Sara can't speak, even to Charles Catz. She gets up and opens a can full of a shredded pink and yellow substance, puts it on his plate, and then goes back to the sofa, to the exact same spot on the cushion, the only place in the world where she can bear to sit. It occurs to her that she doesn't even know where Jonah is. She doesn't know if he's been arrested, if he's in jail, if he's with the Other Wife. Or if the Other Wife is in jail.

Charles Catz struts across the room, licking his catly chops. He springs up on the sofa and steps onto her lap, circles around until his tail is in her face, and begins to knead her thighs, purring loudly. She doesn't stop him, no matter how far through her jeans he thrusts his claws, how deep they dig into her flesh.

Sara has long been a proponent of the

butterfly's wing theory of fate. She doesn't believe in coincidence; she believes that there's a reason for everything, including death and destruction and broken shoelaces and rain. It comforts her to believe that the events that occur in the universe are not random. *If there were no guiding force, how could people live in this world?* She believes that each person has a job to do on this planet.

Sometimes, of course, it's hard to figure out what that job might be, or what step Fate, God, or the Great Spirit desires you to take next. For instance, Sara has been trying for a very long time to figure out what should happen to the relationship she has with Jonah, to whom she has been married for nearly fifteen years. She's given up on what she and Jonah started to do so long ago – they no longer keep goats or farm more than pot-raised cherry tomatoes, she invests what she can in a mutual fund for her old age, they have cell phones. These things are all tiny dribs and little drabs, but they add up, and they have completely undermined the old firmly chosen life until it is gone, and nothing but the shell of the original Sara remains.

Sara supposes that she still loves Jonah, in the way that people settle for after they lose hope. She isn't an unhappy person; but if terrorists seized one of those jets soaring overhead and aimed it at her roof, is Jonah the person with whom she would choose to die? Would Jonah show any heroism as the end approached?

Not that Sara insists on heroism. As far as she's concerned, it takes constant heroism simply to continue to live in this world. Work, suffering, luck: it amounts to a full-time job for every available guardian angel. Hers seems to be on sabbatical at the moment.

But maybe not. Maybe she's cupped like a
tame English sparrow in her guardian angel's
hands, carried unknowing like a prize from place to
place, safe and warm but living a life completely
wrong for someone of her species.

"What I need," Sara says aloud, "is a *deus
ex machina*." At least, she *thinks* that's what she
needs. *Deus ex machina, black box, figure in the
carpet*; she isn't sure about the meaning of any of
those things. September 1970, first day of Chem
110: *It is happening inside a black box*, Professor
Cronin announced, and she panicked. *What* is
happening? All around her people were assiduously
recording the words of Professor Cronin, while
Sara was lost outside of the *black box*. She needed
a *deus ex machina* then, too, a sudden little god
who would descend from above and explain.

Supposing one came now, ejected from a
transcontinental jet and drifting down past Watkins
Butte, wafting first this way, then that, on the
gentle currents of air that rise from the valley in
late afternoon. *What you should do*, the little god
would say, *is...*

The god wouldn't be able to think of
anything either.

Just as it did yesterday, the phone rings and
Charles Catz stops kneading. Together Sara and
Charles Catz watch the phone as it rings, and then,
when, the message machine clicks on, Charles
circles and flops down on her lap.

"Just wondering." It's Melrita's sing-song
voice, the one she thinks hides her ulterior motives.
Just won-da-ring. "Just wondering if you've seen
any of his Mexicans around." In this case, Sara
knows, *he* refers to their mutual neighbor, the
grape-grower. "He's got some of them up from

California. Just don't worry, if you see them, they can be pretty sly but just let them know you know who they are. Bye-bye."

For two days nothing more happens, but on the third day Jonah's picture is on the front page of the morning paper under a headline reading LOCAL ENVIRONMENTALIST ARRESTED.

That particular photograph has been used before, inside, in the *Living* section, under a different headline: LOCAL ENTREPRENEUR PROFITS FROM NATURE'S BOUNTY. In researching that story Joanne Farrigut, the reporter, had called the library for information on blue-green algae, which Jonah's company was selling, and Sara took the call. Joanne Farrigut ended up not using anything Sara found.

But in the course of her research Sara had discovered that blue-green algae wasn't algae at all; it was *cyanobacterium*, a type of bacteria.

"What about truth in advertising?" she'd said when she came home that night.

"Oh, sure," Jonah had said. "'Eat bacteria and you'll be healthy!'"

"It works for yogurt," she said.

"Yogurt is pure white and straight out of Elsie," Jonah said. "This is pond scum."

The week after the company got their first order, from northern California, *E. coli* was found in the lake where they harvested their product, and that was the end of that.

Every day for more than two weeks there is another tidbit in the news. Some members of the board of directors of KindErth are interviewed: *they had no idea. They trusted Jonah McDonald.*

Several articles state that the two Wives apparently knew nothing about McDonald's nefarious activities. It is believed, the articles say, that neither wife was aware of the other's existence.

Some of the evidence is made public: over the past two years Jonah has spent more than $18,000 on jewelry and another $4,322 on women's underwear. He has spent thousands upon thousands of dollars at Powell's City of Books in Portland, where he and his wife (*not this wife!* Sara thinks) are known bibliophiles. And thousands more dollars have disappeared; *spent,* she supposes, *on the Other Wife's mortgage, the Other Wife's living room furniture, the Other Wife's haircuts and manicures and massages.*

A long article on the *e. coli* in the blue-green algae runs on the front page under the headline *HOW MUCH DID JONAH KNOW?*

Sara forces herself to read everything. She saves every issue of the newspaper, though she can't bring herself to cut out the articles and paste them into a scrapbook, as she sometimes has an urge to do. There will never be anyone to look at the scrapbook in the future; she and Jonah have no children who will ever need or want to know the truth.

She doesn't answer the telephone for many days. She looks out the window as it rings, her heartbeat roughening as the message machine picks up, and then she hears either a silence, a click, and the hum of the empty line, or a voice.

"Mrs. McDonald?" They start like that. A man from Channel Ten calls a lot. Someone claiming to be from *People* magazine calls. JoAnne Farrigut, no doubt regretting her original carelessness about *cyanobacterium*, calls every evening for a week. But Sara doesn't pick up the phone.

Melrita calls every day. "Did you hear those gunshots last night?" she says to the machine. "Don't worry, they were on the other side of the hill."

Another time, she says, "Don't worry, I'm keeping the gate locked up *tight*."

And, "Listen, I know you don't care for it, but don't you worry, some people pray."

Finally Sara calls Melrita back. Melrita never answers her phone, either, but Sara is sure that Melrita is listening as she leaves a message. "Melrita, it's Sara," she says. "Thanks for keeping an eye on the gate."

Jonah is arraigned. He pleads guilty. The judge says he is not a danger to society and releases him from jail for a large amount of money.

The Board of KindErth says that they certainly hope McDonald will pay back the money he stole from them, but even if he paid it now, at once, in full, they would still press charges. This was a violation of trust, one man is quoted as saying solemnly, perhaps on the verge of tears. This crime cannot go unpunished.

Sara had come west right after college, and she lived around California with first one boy, then another, until suddenly years had flown. (Time has that habit, of slipping slyly away without saying good-bye.) When she moved north (with a boyfriend whose name she now has trouble retrieving) she felt that it was in the nick of time; and sure enough, not long afterwards she met

Jonah. He was not someone she would ever have called *the love of her life*, but he was smart – he had gone to Reed College – and he was tall and he agreed with her politically and philosophically on how life should be lived. That is, he agreed that while we are not here simply to have a good time, we are not here to accrue wealth or prestige or items, either. That the meaning of life lies in the living of it, in the moments between conscious plans. Jonah was unembarrassed by the trust fund from his nuclear engineer father, and sometimes even grumbled about it.

"It isn't big enough to give away, or establish a foundation, or buy a mansion on the coast," he had said one afternoon as they lay on his rumpled sheets listening to the cars pass along the wet street outside the window.

"But it's a good hedge, isn't it?" she said. "It's a help?"

"It's hardly worth having," Jonah said. "I just spend it."

That was before, and now it is after. How can Sara bear to face the world? How can she go to work? But of course she must, since it's clear that from now on Sara will be without Jonah's trust fund, his salary or the embezzled money from KindErth (which *she* never saw a cent of).

The people at the library are kind people, in general, and they try to be kind to her. Whoever is on the front desk keeps an eye out for reporters, and Alma lends Sara to the Processing department "for the time being," so she won't have to face the public.

But this situation is worse than death! At least with death you can check with Ann Landers on the rules: you say you're sorry, you go to a

memorial service in the children's department, you
bring a casserole, you walk the dead man's faithful
dog, you give a book in memory of the deceased.
But embezzlement is stupid! Bigamy is funny!
Such dumb crimes! One can understand a mistress
– what man doesn't have a mistress? – but why
would someone as smart as Jonah bother to go
through a sham wedding ceremony?

"You must be in shock," Don says to her in
the staff lounge. He hands her a cup of machine
coffee and turns back to get one for himself. "I
wish there were something I could do."

But there's nothing anyone can do! Sara's
on her own. No one can *turn back the hands of time*
and no one can make her feel better and no one can
give her back a life which turns out to have been a
complete waste of time, energy, and hope.

Once, on her lunch hour, she searches
Google for *Jonah McDonald* and gets a wealth of
hits. Stories about his foolish crimes, but a few
others, too: KindErth annual reports. The Blue-
green Algae Development, Inc., website, still up
but long out of date. Even a story about his father,
Maxwell McDonald, and the nuclear device he
patented in 1963. It refers in passing to *his son,
Jonah, an environmental entrepreneur.*

She searches on *Sara McDonald* and in
addition to the embezzlement stories she finds
herself on the library's Website, getting a pin as a
20-year employee. She also discovers that she
might be a fiction writer, a botanist, a florist in
Tallahassee, a high school soccer star, a cellist, and
the star of an independent film that won an award
at Sundance.

Sara McDonald, fool.

———

There is so much work to do! and with Jonah gone Sara has to do it all. She splits kindling and brings in firewood and takes out garbage and buys groceries and feeds Charles Catz and reads the electric meter and pays the phone bill and stokes the stove morning and night. But although it's a lot to do, at no time does it seem impossible, or incorrect, or unfair, or as if she hasn't been doing it all along. It's as if Jonah had never been there.

She *does* miss him now and then; she misses the sound of the toilet flushing in the morning, of someone watching football on a Monday night, the feeling, at the end of the afternoon, that someone will soon come up the driveway and into the house. She misses another presence in the house, another coat thrown on a coat hook or taken down, a second pair of muddy boots in the mudroom. She sometimes thinks for a split second that someone is out on the property, turning the compost or testing the shakiness of a fencepost. Sometimes when she wakes up in the night she lies very still before she remembers that turning on the light to read for a while will wake up no one. Charles Catz can sleep through anything.

In recent years Sara had found herself more and more interested in serious things. She's tired of being entertained, and of looking for pleasure, and of going to places where worries won't go. She *wants* worries; she wants to feed the hungry, clothe the naked, and read aloud to small children whose parents never do. Just how to go about changing her life so that it's composed of these things she is unsure. She's astonished that so much of her life has already passed without leaving much of a trace, either in the world itself or in her.

When she finally realized, not so very long ago, that she would not have children, something in her slipped away. Not having children wasn't a tragedy, it was a decision she had made over and over again for most of her life; but when it was clear that a door had closed behind her while she wasn't paying attention, and no more doors would be opening into that room *ever*, she was taken by surprise. In fact, she was shocked. She sank down into herself, into a small dark shape huddled in the bottom of her own soul. It was the first real thing that had ever happened to her.

"What's the point of living if you never *do* anything?" she had said to Jonah.

"What difference would it make?" he asked. "You live a while and then you die. What goes in between is irrelevant." He was carefully emptying a bowl of Cheerios, eating them one at a time.

"You're depressed, aren't you," she'd said.

"Honey," Jonah had said without looking up, "you're the depressed one. You'll get over it, but don't ask me how."

Then a few other things happened: her father got sick and died, after what seemed years but was really only a few long months of trouble. Her mother also died (and left some money that Sara has put into her IRA). Then the bigamy thing.

Sara suspects that she is free now; that there is nothing to tie her down and so nothing to weigh her down, nothing to keep her from – there's the rub: *from what?* The thing that will soon happen. Surely most things that happen now will be happening for good. The small dark shape will lift its head, and stretch, and with a yawn stand up and look around. Out of the black box.

It isn't until a rainy evening in February that she comes home from work to find things missing. A hat is gone from the rack in the mudroom, a painting has disappeared from the hall. She hurries through room after room, yanking open drawers and doors. A chair, the good camera, the clothes from his closet. The *dishes?* A complete set of dishes! There was nothing special about them; they were stoneware from Fred Meyer, a dime a dozen, the same things on half the kitchen tables in Oregon. Why would he take the dishes?

She panics. She runs into the living room and drops to her knees to look under the sofa, runs upstairs and looks at the bed, under the bed, in the linen closet in the bathroom. On the bottom shelf of the linen closet is Charles Catz, curled up on a purple towel and glaring at her.

"Oh, thank god," she says. Charles closes his eyes and tucks his nose back between his feet, and Sara begins to cry. She sits down on the edge of the bathtub and cries for a long time, unable to stop.

To think that Jonah has abandoned Charles Catz, who loves him.

In December more traffic goes up and down their shared driveway than in all the years Sara has lived here. Several times she has to back up and wait for a line of cars – from California, from Idaho, from Nevada – to go past her. All of Melrita's children have come home for Christmas for the first time in eighteen years, because their father, Cuthbert, who lives in town, is dying. They spend the afternoons sitting with him in the hospital and come back to Melrita's at night.

Whenever they're all out of the house –

there are four daughters, two sons-in-law, and three or four grown-up grandchildren – Melrita calls Sara.

"It's right for them to see him," she says. "All those years he never would pay any attention to them, and then she – " Melrita means the second wife – "wouldn't even let him talk to them on the phone. Now, well, he looks awful."

"He's quite ill?" Sara says.

"Oh, he's bad. I only know because Mishele tells me. The others don't tell me much but she has to talk."

"Melrita," Sara says, "I'm going to visit a friend in New York for New Year's. I'll be gone a week."

"New York?" Melrita's voice goes high and shy. "Aren't you afraid to fly there? All that."

"Well, I figure if God wants me, he'll find me wherever I am," Sara says. It's *sort* of how she feels, except for the God part.

Melrita laughs, which is what Sara had hoped for. "That is really, really true," she says. "Look at *him*. He hid from God as long as he could."

"He must be glad to see the girls again," Sara says.

"Well, I don't know," Melrita says, sounding thoughtful. "He's pretty far gone. It might not matter to him now. I don't know, I haven't seen him since the day he left the house. You want me to feed that cat?"

"If you would," Sara says. "I sure would appreciate it."

"I like cats," Melrita says. "I may get another one some time. I'll pray for your airplane."

"Thanks, Melrita," Sara says. "Have a

happy new year."

Sara is standing in line waiting to go through airport security when she sees Dana Sheffield ahead of her, just walking through the metal detector. The alarm sounds and Dana stops, lifting her hands. The guard motions her back through the frame, where she searches the pockets of her jacket and pulls out a set of keys. She takes off a watch, then unbuckles her belt, and places everything in the little plastic bin the guard hands her. She passes through the gate again, and the alarm is silent.

On the other side, Sara looks around and finally spots Dana Sheffield sitting on the far side of the crowded room, reading a Kindle. She is certainly well-groomed. Her short hair is casually tossed, the ends tipped with silver, and even from across the room Sara can see that her neatly-pressed clothes lack pills and cat hair. Dana suddenly looks up from her Kindle and Sara glances away. When she looks back, Dana Sheffield is staring once again at the Kindle.

On the plane, Dana, already settled and immersed again in her Kindle, doesn't look up as Sara passes through First Class to reach her own seat. If she were someone else, or if things were different, Sara would have reached down to touch Dana's shoulder. "Hey there, stranger," she would have said. Or, "Dana Sheffield, isn't it?" But she isn't, and they aren't, and she doesn't. She shoves her bag into the overhead storage bin and squeezes into her seat beside the window, where she takes out her own book (*The Poisonwood Bible,* which she's been meaning to read for years). She can see the side of Dana Sheffield's well-groomed head, an ear, a swath of hair draped casually over the temple. Elegant reading glasses. A thin shoulder clad in a bright rosy sweater – cashmere, no doubt.

Sara shakes her head, amused at herself. What did Dana Sheffield ever do to her, that Sara can only find fault with her? Been suckered into believing Jonah, just like everyone else? No, it's just that Dana Sheffield is one of the few people Sara knows who has met both wives. That's all. *As she was going to St. Ives, she'd met both of Jonah's wives.*

Maybe Dana was the whistle-blower! Maybe, her curiosity stirred by the strange wife situation, Dana had begun to ask questions. Had casually, in the course of a meeting of the KindErth Board of Directors, asked about some questionable expenditures. *What about these receipts from Powell's City of Books, Jonah? Sara Paretsky, Patricia Cornwall, Louise Erdrich – for an organization devoted to teaching children nonconfrontational environmental advocacy? Can you explain?*

By the end of the flight Sara feels almost bold enough to ask her. But when they land in San Francisco, and she finally makes her way out of the plane and into the terminal, Dana Sheffield is nowhere in sight. No doubt she's going into the city for the weekend, to shop, or to attend a reception for the rich at the public library. Sara heads for her connecting flight.

Sara's been to New York before: when she was fairly young she flew there to visit a man she had hoped was someone she would come to love, but she knew the instant she came up the ramp into the terminal and saw the moving sidewalk carrying him toward her that he wasn't. They had a pleasant enough weekend, though. He took her to the opera, albeit to something German and to seats in the last row of the highest balcony. And when they saw a sandwich board reading *PHOTO EXHIBIT*, they wandered into a gallery even he hadn't known was there, and what should be inside up a flight of stairs but photographs of the moon by Ansel Adams! Later, in a bright, under-heated restaurant they ate beautifully arranged foods on colorful Fiestaware (this was just before Fiestaware came back into vogue). But both nights she lay awake all night in his icy corner room above Riverside Drive listening to the single-paned window rattle in the wind. Now and then a gust lifted the window shade enough to let the light from the street shoot in like a camera flash, and with every passing minute she grew hungrier and colder, waiting for dawn.

All that business with Jonah and the embezzling and the bigamy – it has turned out to have almost nothing to do with her. And she has never seen him again, *not since the day he left the house.* Imagine that! After fifteen years of marriage, one day her husband was just gone, and she never saw him again, and she doesn't even want to. Aaron has told her – Aaron Blake, the lawyer she hired to handle her divorce – that Jonah was last heard of managing a landfill operation for a county government in Florida.

"What about her?" Sara says.

Aaron says he doesn't know.

Of course Sara won't get any of Jonah's money; she didn't try to, and anyway his trust fund is inviolable. Not even KindErth can get at that. Aaron assumes Jonah's wages at the landfill in Florida are garnisheed, but they can't amount to much.

Sara had worried that as Jonah's legal wife she might be held responsible for his debts, but Aaron successfully guided her through a maze of public declarations of non-responsibility.

"The bigamy thing played in your favor," he said. "In the public eye."

Ardith looks terrific, though a little thicker through the hips and with frosty streaks in her black hair. She's Ivan's third wife.

"He had a regular life with a regular wife, that's Sam's mother," she tells Sara on the way in from the airport, through traffic so terrifying the only sight Sara can see is a vision of her own death. "Then he got a blonde trophy wife who broke his heart. And now he's got me. The consolation wife."

Ardith and Ivan take Sara all around New York. Thank god, it's warmer than when she visited the man she never came to love. They go to the Statue of Liberty and to a concert at Lincoln Center, and they wait in line for a long time to stand on a platform overlooking Ground Zero. Ivan knew a number of people who died in the attack, engineers and stockbrokers and quite a few secretaries.

"Whenever I come by here," he tells Sara, "I stop and I consciously think about one of them. Just one at a time. Superstition, really. Means nothing to them, of course. But I've always thought it would be rather unfair to die *en masse*. War, epidemics, disaster. Much better to have a death of your own."

Can that be true? Is it more satisfying to die if you think the big finger is pointing right at you? As if the forces that make these decisions – *birth, death, infinity* – have all turned to look at you, and glance back at each other, nodding, indicating agreement that *her time is now*. To be the focus of all attention: is that what one would want in one's last moments?

Or would there be comfort in companionship, the knowledge that you are in the same boat with, say, a hundred, a thousand, a million others? Some of those people died helping each other down the stairs. Would that be a comfort, to be holding the hand of a stranger in a dark stairwell when the end arrives?

What Sara will remember forever about the days after the attack is the silence, the stillness deeper than a Sunday afternoon, the regained dominion of birds over the skies and the air, the careless way they flitted from pine to tube feeder to cosmos and out into the oaks. A hundred years could pass and she would remember that silent sky.

Melrita had called Sara four times that day and twice a day afterwards for a week, to make sure the gate was locked and to ask Sara if she'd seen any Mexicans lurking around. "With that dark skin," she'd said, "you don't know *what* their religion is."

Sara closes her eyes. The air is amazingly soft for December in New York, and the sun lies heavily on her cheeks. Ivan is, really, a lovely man. He's just what Sara had hoped: tall, still quite straight, white-moustached, courtly. Plus, he's thoughtful and he isn't afraid to express his emotions. Sara loves the way he treats Ardith, as if she's a brilliant *artiste*.

"She needs her space," he said the first morning, when Ardith had gone to her studio and left them at the breakfast table. "And her time. She does remarkable work. Remarkable." He took a sip of the strong coffee, and the delicate white china cup clattered just a little as he replaced it on its saucer. "To think I spent my whole life trying to find a woman I could really love. Seventy-three years!"

He leaned back in the chair and gazed at the pattern in the royal blue carpet, then looked up and smiled at Sara. "Well, okay, maybe only sixty," he said, as if she'd talked him down, although she had said nothing. "For the first thirteen it was my mother I loved. And then – " He lifted his hands in amazement. "Everything changed!"

POPEYE'S THEOREM

Sometimes I forget my name. I use it so rarely, and I act as myself so rarely, that I have lost any sense that I am anyone at all. I'm not saying this to be morose or pitiful or to stir in you alarm that I'm despondent or on the verge of something. It's just something I've noticed, and marvel at: I make a phone call, say, and when I hear myself give my name I marvel that I was able to remember it.

Claude knew his name as soon as he woke up. He didn't know the president, but he was never much interested in politics anyway; he never believed it relevant to him. When asked about his dog he remembered good old Zipper, who died in 1993. He remembered his address and telephone number from the house we lived in when he was nine. He remembered me, his big sister, and he remembered his mother's name – Mom – and his father's – Dad. He remembered the names of several of the friends who later forsook him.

Then things get murky. It's hard to tell what he's forgotten and what he just can't manage to do. Brush his teeth, for instance. Maybe he just refuses to remember to do it because it's too hard for him. You remind him and he slaps his forehead and says *Oh yeah!* In a minute or two you say Claude, the teeth? Whap! *Oh yeah.* And he struggles up from whatever chair he's in and shuffles to the bathroom, and sometimes he remembers to put toothpaste on the brush and sometimes he doesn't, but either way he dutifully brushes his teeth for twenty or thirty minutes, or until you remind him to stop.

I do not blame – well, no, not true, I *do* blame the boys, the men, who have forsaken my brother. But I understand them fully. I myself would forsake him if he were someone else's brother. How many people in the world will continue to give time and attention to a person who no longer has a concept of time and whose attention span was blown to smithereens in a distant desert town?

If Claude and I had grown old together we might have become better friends. My mother has told me that she and her sisters were not particular friends in childhood, and after high school they went their separate ways, but by the time death and disappointment and the diminution of hormones had made inroads into their lives in their fifties, they had become fast friends and confidantes. They clung together in the face of death.

There, look what I said. *If we had grown old together.* Here we both are, chugging through the years, which is called aging; yet something is happening to me that is not happening to him.

On the other hand, what has happened to him has very definitely happened to me.

Here's what happened. I was home visiting my parents. The phone rang. I understand that when it's a fatality they have to come to the door.

By twos, like Mormons. If it's not fatal they can let you know by phone.

The phone rang and my father answered it. I was sitting in the living room reading. I was reading Jhumpa Lahiri. She writes the sort of story that makes me nervous, because I know someone is going to do something wrong. Not murder, not a big unlikely thing, but a big foolish thing, something that I might do. The sort of thing I *have* done and could tell you about in detail, except that I prefer not to think of any of those things. I know what it's like to do a big little terrible thing, but I turn out the light in that room of my brain when I happen to open the door.

But her writing is so beautiful, so easy, that I love to read it. If only nothing ever happened in her stories!

The phone rang. My father answered it. I am a nosy person, I was listening to him. *Hello?* he said. He was so pathetic, and I don't like thinking of my father as pathetic. One's father should be strong and smart. He answered the fucking phone! His voice was helpless!

I see, said my father. *Yes. Yes. Yes, we'll be here all day. Please let us know. Please – wait, who can I call? No, but. Yes.* He motioned to me, wildly waving his hand, *bring it, bring it*, then pinched his fingers together and made a writing motion. I scrambled up from the sofa and ran into the kitchen for a pen and ran back. I had no paper. I wrote on the lampshade as my father repeated the numbers. A telephone number.

When he hung up he shouted, "Martha!"

We heard her faint voice.

"Martha!" he shouted again.

"In a minute," she called.

He reached for the pen and put it in his shirt pocket.

The numbers are still on the lampshade. I turned them toward the wall. I don't know if my parents know they're there. I don't know if they'd know what the numbers are. I know.

The toilet flushed and the bathroom door opened so that the flushing was louder and my mother came down the stairs.

Just as she got to the bottom my father said, "Martha, Claude's been injured."

She put a hand on the banister and said, "How badly."

My father's voice broke when he answered that one. "They don't know," he said. "He's just going into surgery right now. In Germany. I think it's bad."

And if the golf cart doesn't head out for lunch with the tea caddy, I'll tell you the story of Daddy and the understatement.

One of these days I'm going to light out, but right now my major preoccupation is finding a decent hairdresser. There are not that many in this town, and of course only a few of them are acceptable to begin with. Say six or eight. Say I get my hair cut every six weeks: that's eight times a year.

I walk in, I sit down in the chair, and the chosen hairdresser looks at my head, looks at my face in the mirror, and says, *Now, what are we doing?*

I describe what I want – *a sort of bob, not square, not in layers, long in the back, and see this piece here? I don't want that to stick up*. She nods and has at it, snipping and snapping away in my

mass of wiry hair. And when I get home I have a
layered head in the shape of a square, chopped right
off at the nape of my neck, with that chunk on the
left side bulging out in the shape of Minnie
Mouse's ear.

I give these poor hairdressers no slack!
Usually I go two or three times before I get fed up
and switch. And of course eventually – there being
so little choice – I have to start over again.

You probably want to know why Claude
enlisted in the first place, what his high school
career was like, how he interacted with his friends,
all of that. Believe me, it's irrelevant.

When you live this way, with someone
suffering from a certain malady, you learn too
much. You learn that there is no time in the day, no
time in our lives, to ponder anything. It is one
damned thing after another, detail piled upon detail,
getting the man out of bed and getting food into
him and waste out of him. Trying to make him feel
worthwhile. Trying to make ourselves feel that
what we are doing is worthwhile.

Claude doesn't play real sports any more
because he is lacking such a large piece of skull
and – horrors! – his brain might get hurt. But every
Friday night he and Denny play video games. I
don't like to admit that it makes me nervous when
he plays them, he gets so excited and waves his arm
and shouts and pounds on things and jumps around
in his chair. His brain might get hurt.

The first time Denny came to the door I
didn't think we should let him in. I thought he'd
come to gawk. He was the older brother of
Claude's former best friend Jeff, and Jeff, after
coming once, had made himself scarce. He had a

job, he had a girlfriend. He was a busy man.

To his credit, Denny didn't make excuses for his brother, and in fact only mentioned his name once, when he first rang the bell. He said he was Jeff's brother, Denny. Could he come in?

Now he comes by once a week and they sit in front of Claude's flatscreen and blow each other up, ramming each other's car off the road. Laughing and hooting, yelling. I know Claude has a good time at it. It's about the only good time he has. If his brain were more intact he'd be waiting at his front door for hours before Denny arrives. As it is, though, and maybe this is some kind of blessing, he can't keep track of the days of the week. Nothing has worked, crossing off squares on the wall calendar, having an electronic device beep at him, nothing. Hours and days mean nothing to him. So he is always pleasantly surprised when Denny shows up at the door with a pizza or buffalo wings from Pizza Hut that they zap in the wave and devour as they kill each other's proxy over and over again.

I'd like to know why Denny comes. I try to put myself in the position he's taken on: friend to a disabled person who has no short-term memory, can't understand the humor in most situations, can't be trusted to cross the street without either dropping his cane or falling to his knees or both, and who occasionally has a seizure which knocks him out of the box for a couple of days afterwards. And to top it off, can't remember your name.

Maybe he's in training for the priesthood, and this is a work of charity. Or maybe he's going to go back to school and study psychology, or write about Posttraumatic Stress Syndrome and Traumatic Brain Injury in Iraq Vets. Maybe he's a secret peacenik – my grandfather's word! – and is collecting data to reveal at a hearing. Maybe he's a pervert and likes being around people of limited mentation. Maybe he's deeply ashamed of his brother's abandonment of my brother and is trying to make it up. Maybe he's in love with me and thinks the way to win my heart is by stuffing my brother's stomach with buffalo wings.

Sometimes I am satisfied with my hair. It all depends on what it looks like when I get up in the morning. There are some mornings, when the humidity is high enough and I haven't slept too long on one side, that it looks great! I feel like a hundred and two bucks! And my search becomes less frantic, less drastic, less a life-and-death situation. On those days I can dress in brighter colors, I dare to wear lipstick, I walk along with my head fairly high. It's all in the hair.

I am one hundred percent sure that Claude, like the others in his vehicle, was concentrating one hundred percent on what he was doing. Inching through enemy territory in a Humvee, keeping all eyes and ears open for signs of explosive devices, for fast or surreptitious movements among the populace, for birds that didn't fly, for dogs that didn't bark in the night. I wonder, if he had stinted on the attention then, would less of it have been exposed to the blast? Would he have retained some of it somewhere deep inside, to be brought out now that he is home and safe and has other things – like his teeth, his video games, the crossing of streets – to pay that attention to?

Anyone just looking at my brother doesn't have a clue that he is not a whole person. That a large part of his brain was slammed and mashed and chopped out so that now, no matter which way a thought goes in Claude's brain, it comes to the edge of an abyss beyond which there is nothing. A black chasm. And his poor little thoughts have no internal resources, they can't backtrack or jump over to another track. Thought after thought stops and dies at the edge of that abyss.

There was a time I could have asked Claude what it was like. Not just the explosion, but being there, in Iraq. We were not particularly close but we were used to each other, we could talk. Not about our deepest desires, not our yearnings, but we could describe pretty accurately and without embarrassment what had happened to us and, often, how we felt about it.

But probably just his being there would have taken that away. The things we could talk about in our teenage years were things that happened in our shared universe of youth and family and sports and jobs and the fucking little town where we lived. Heading out in armored vehicles to play dodge 'em with explosive devices was not within the realm of our shared experiences. I don't think that even at his most articulate he could have described it to me. He probably liked some aspects of it, and I wouldn't have been able to understand that. Adrenaline played a different role in his life than in mine.

If only he were pitiful, pitiable. You know, a pathetic, weak individual who lies abed gazing at flowers. It's just really hard to feel affection for a crass 13-year-old boy with no depth. Who can't do his share of the chores because he can't understand how to do them. Or that he should do them. Or that there are chores in the world to be done.

It reflects on me, of course. I should be

able to abide him because after all he is my brother and he has never done anything to hurt me. Except close his mind to me, ha ha!

If he were a vegetable.

If he were totally crippled.

If he had died.

Then I would be able to feel some affection for him.

Love is not love that alters when it alteration finds.

Yeah, well. Love cannot help but alter in some cases.

Now and then I try a new hairdresser. More often than not I *love* what she does for the first hour. I *love* it. Kicky, cute, easy; makes me feel 40 pounds lighter and a couple of cities more sophisticated. By the next morning it makes me look like I'm carrying a death's head at the top of my neck. It will take another three years to get back to where I was yesterday at this time, a shaggy thick curtain of hair hanging heavy around my jaw. I thought it weighed me down so I wanted it shortened, but this cut reveals far too much of my body and of my soul.

I believe what I've said about Claude here doesn't do his intellect justice. He does have aspirations. He would like to have a job.

He would like to be able to have a job.

He would benefit by having some concept of what a job is.

He was never going to be a nuclear physicist, but he wasn't a stupid boy. He majored in biology. He could have done something in the health sciences. I like to think he might have become an EMT. Or an orderly, one of those calm, strong, understanding orderlies who intuit what their patients are suffering and know how to calm them and how to reach the silent unreachable ones.

Well, *that* went blooey in Iraq! This Claude can't tell when his own mother is upset. He snickers when he sees her crying. He can't carry a stretcher because his grip is unreliable. He has a strong fist, but around a handle it's liable to drift open as he concentrates on walking. Can't have an orderly who can't hold on to the patient's gait belt. Whose grasp on the bedpan is questionable.

His givens are different now. We have learned to divide these things up not in a hierarchical way but solely on a timeline.

Birth through 23: basic good looks, good health, moderate athletic ability that will provide a pastime throughout life, a reasonable ability to maintain a loving relationship with a potential mate, headed for a career in the health care field.

23 to the present, and beyond: ability to walk with a cane, ability to maintain a semi-independent living situation with aides and supervision. Someday perhaps some kind of wage-earning job in a rote, assembly-line set-up.

I didn't go up to Bethesda with them when they first went, I wasn't there when they walked through the door of my brother's room to find a bald man with a melon head and black eyes and plastic tubing running into orifices where no orifices were before. A lump of a man who gurgled. Who gurgled as he slept through the first three weeks they were with him. As they sat in terror beside his bed, not knowing who would be there when – if – his eyes opened.

They did open, and it was a disabled

Claude. An unabled Claude.

Or, as we now prefer, a differently abled Claude. I appreciate the terminology at last, not in support of his dignity but as an attempt by his family to live in the present. We are all trying to Be Here Now.

Same with this awful, awful haircut! It doesn't matter what my hair looked like when I was sixteen or what vision I carried of myself and my future in the past, this hair is what I now have! It will grow at its own rate, and I can have no control; I must make my way through this world beneath this head of hair. It is my given. Not me. But me now.

The worst thing? It blew away his sense of humor! God, it's like something out of Ursula K. LeGuin! He laughs, but it's the wrong laugh. Sounds like a song, doesn't it? *He laughs, but it's the wrong laugh.* It's not from humor but from something in his brain that wasn't there before; or from a shadow of something that was there but is gone. The explosion whacked his brain but what it blew away was his soul.

I used to be funny myself. I used to find humor in just about everything. I wrote funny stories and pointed out amusing arrangements of words on signs. I caught the mistaken meanings people assign to words and the misspellings in the world around me. No longer, though. I am dulled and dimmed by what has happened to my brother. I am draped with survivor's guilt, great heavy velveteen swathes of it.

You know how, when you associate a
certain piece of music with a certain event or place
or time, you can never hear that music again
without it getting in the way of your life? My
brother is like that, like a piece of music. We may
not have been close but I associate him with my
whole life, including my aspirations. I was going to
go far and do many things, and become a patent
attorney or a cellist or run a half-way house for
abused women.

Now I'm incapable of sustained attention
to anything. I can hardly think one day ahead
except to schedule some health care-related event.
Sometimes I can do nothing but stare out the
window at the poor damned birds dashing to the
feeder to seize seeds in between snowflakes, which
at the moment are falling hot and heavy – ha ha! –
through the universe. Stare at the cars going by,
whose drivers peer into my yard and at my
window, maliciously hoping to spy on me. Stare at
my walls, at framed photographs and little art prints
that mean nothing to me any more, not even when I
shake myself out of my stupor and consciously *look*
at them, thinking of where they came from and why
I have them there, of the dead people and animals
portrayed in them, at the creatures who never lived
yet achieved immortality by appearing to thresh
some wheat or dance with a bearded man or howl
at a moon that is rising orange behind a snow-laden
fir.

To make up for my inability to concentrate,
I'm trying to learn not to despair quite so much. It
has involved the scaling down of any number of
dreams and goals into which I won't go right now.
They're too embarrassing. Let it suffice to say that
I have adopted Popeye's Theorem: I yam what I

yam.

You'd think I would have figured this out some time ago. That it wouldn't take the ruination of my brother's brain to make me face myself.

I know I make this sound, I have made all of this sound, as if I am the one who suffers. In truth, I am way down the line in the suffering hierarchy. Claude would be first, if I could believe that he understands enough to suffer. He has lost his former life, including its future. That's a biggy. But if he doesn't know that – well, maybe it doesn't hurt him.

Claude's mother? Pow! Her heart is riddled with the fragments of her boy's brain, her present life and her future all sucked into Taking Care of Claude. When she is awake, her mind is on him. When she's asleep, god knows where her mind goes. She used to tell us her dreams; at the breakfast table as the sun streamed in the windows we laughed over coffee and coffeecake at the tableaux in which she had found herself the night before, and at the hilarious nonsequitors issuing from the lips of long-dead relatives or distant celebrities.

No dreams now. No laughter from Claude or from me, though she tries gamely now and then to entertain us. Sorry, Mom, doesn't work, back to your grief.

As for Dad, he's earning as many bucks as he can before he's too old. He goes out the door to the car in the morning and he works all day, and he comes home and sits with his son at the dinner table, surreptitiously reaching over now and then to push Claude's plate away from the table edge or to put a piece of chicken back on the plate or to hand

Claude a napkin to wipe his chin – Claude won't stand being wiped but he obediently wipes when you hand him a napkin.

In fact we are lucky, *luckyluckylucky!* in many, *many* regards, in that way!

1. Claude wipes with no urging when you tell him to! Lips, chin, rear end, he follows the instruction when you hand him the tissue and indicate its destination.

2. He has lost his taste for alcohol! I understand that alcohol would render his anti-seizure medication ineffective, or enhance its effects, causing stupor or narcolepsy or irrational agitation. But when given a beer or something else by mistake, Claude grimaces and shoves it the hell away. For Claude, traumatic brain injury is as good as Antibuse!

3. Claude is not prone to violence! or even to anger, really. He's just stupid, coarse, lethargic, and humorless now. He lurches, he doesn't bathe without a reminder, he can't bait his own hook, and he doesn't hold up his end of a conversation. But, except in his video games, he *isn't violent!*

He isn't violent, and that's a lucky thing for us!

Not too long ago, having run through my selected options, I went back to a hairdresser whose actual name is Cherish, a bright-faced and cheerfully loud woman. I told her what I wanted this time: *a bit of shaping, softer around the face, not chopped away from my temples.* She pondered my head, lifted and considered a couple of locks, and began snipping with abandon. She chattered away about her daughter who married the insurance

salesman, and the other one, doing ever so well in
college, and about the sundry things a hairdresser
can go on about while she goes about her business,
which is my head. At the end she stood back and
presented me to myself and I put on my glasses and
considered the cut, which was about what I
expected and not what I'd hoped for.

As I stood at the counter writing a check
she said, "How's your brother doing?"

I was pleased that she remembered. "You
have a good memory," I said. "I guess he's a little
better than he was."

"He's alive," she said, taking my money.
"That's a blessing."

Lately we've had very cold winters, global
warming notwithstanding. This winter, for instance,
it snowed the week before Christmas, the deepest
snow we've had in thirty years, and then the
temperature dropped to zero, freezing the snow in
place. This weather is bad for Claude, who has
trouble getting around because his balance is shot
and his vision is partial, and for us, who help
Claude go places and sometimes have to pick him
up if he falls or stop him from getting out of the car
when there's a pool of slush outside the door.

What these winters have been surprisingly
good for is birding. This year's Christmas Bird
Count, though cold enough to freeze a proverbial
off anything, was made infinitely easier by the
snow. Birds show up like nobody's business
against a pure white background. Bundled up in my
old down coat, which had hung forlornly in a bag
in the attic for ten years but rose bravely to the task
when called up, I stalked the fields and copses of
my assigned area seeking out the little brown

jobbers, and counted the herds of robins devouring the dried fruits on the wild cherry trees, and estimated the number of starlings on the communications tower at the gas company, and I would huddle with my back to the wind and take off a mitten and write down my sightings.

> *North American Robins 89*
> *Eastern bluebirds 3*
> *Red-bellied woodpecker 1*
> *Dark-eyed Juncos 7*
> *White-throated sparrows 5*
> *Eastern Towhee 1*
> *European Starlings 803*

People used to shoot these birds in order to count them, to understand them, even just to see them clearly. Imagine that, imagine shooting them out of the skies by the thousands, birds falling around you like warm-blooded sleet, blanketing your field in feathers and gore, one by one their cries and calls and songs going silent. In the silence you step carefully among them, nudging one small body aside with the toe of your shoe, crushing another underfoot despite your care, kneeling down to pick up a White-throated Sparrow that still breathes, its eye open, a line of blood trickling from the corner of its bill. Gently you crush its neck between your thumb and finger until its eye dulls and its little head falls back against your bright mitten, and you drop it to the ground among the other feathered dead, and rise to walk again.

In any life there are defining moments. Sometimes you recognize them when they happen, sometimes you don't. Sometimes it's an absolute starburst of light in your chest, a thrill that rushes from heart to spine to ribs to xyphoid process and lifts you right into heaven, or at least onto the gently waving limb of a mature elm in midsummer. Other times it slides like a knife into your small intestine, whose contents begin to seep into your peritoneal cavity, and your abdomen blooms heavy and hot with a kind of dull, angry, fatal despair.

Cherish has done my hair wrong, wrong, wrong again, chopped at it until it is a coarse haggard mess not beginning to approach the vision I had for myself. She has no clue. If I could I would pick up a gun and aim it at her stupid face and shoot. I would kneel down in the snow and push the cold heavy barrel into my temple, into that dent in my skull behind my right eye where the bone is so thin, *another blessing!* I lay it against that sorry useless pane of bone and in one fast instant *fast* I squeeze and with a sound like *tsk!* in blood and gobs of brain and laughing shards of sharp white bone I blow my endless thoughts away.

WALK IN THE DARK

Every exit is an entry somewhere else.
— Tom Stoppard

"Shock and awe!" Richard shouts. He whacks the chicken breast with the rolling pin again and again, until the breast is as thin as a fat crepe, as thin as the brim of a baseball cap, as flat and thin as the one comic book he ever owned, *The Twelve Dancing Princesses*.

The shouting is just for effect. He wants to know what it feels like. But the chicken will be excellent.

"I want a useful pet," Richard says, standing in front of the wood stove, his hands in the front pockets of his pale jeans. "Not one of these fawning things." He gazes at the hopeful retriever stretched on the rug in front of him. "Raise it on my own grass, get it professionally whacked and butchered, and keep its parts in my own freezer, to last me through the winter."

"Blue ribbon at the county fair?" Chip asks.

"Absodamnlutely," Richard says, and his

glasses rise slightly on the bridge of his nose.

Watching him strut in front of the stove, Annis thinks *He's no spring chicken.* Richard's fair skin wrinkled years ago, dried up and began to fall off in small patches that leave raw wounds on his face and arms. He is one of those whose youthful freckles spread and flowed into each other, becoming one mottled mass of brown in the background of his blushes.

Richard moves slowly through the vegetables. He eyes each bin of onions, every box of artichokes shrewdly, his upper lip set ready to sneer. It is not for nothing that he worked the law for thirty years; he has dealt with so many criminals, so many petty thieves and armed liars, that he is well aware of what percentage of humanity is out for blood. No one is going to put anything over on him in the vegetable department. He is looking for *broccolini*, and no one can tell him that immature broccoli is just as good.

He talks big. Sometimes he imagines that he is the most violent of men, a thick-muscled wrestler, a Green Beret, a vindictive judge with a lifetime seat on the appellate court. He imagines himself into desires and beliefs that, in reality, would never cross the threshold of his brain. Here he is, far, far into his sixties, and still he is pretending to be what he never will be. Unsure of what he is.

Richard is walking on the logging road with Annis when her retriever comes down out of the woods holding something tucked into his mouth. "Drop it!" Annis says sternly. The good dog lowers his head and works his muzzle, and out falls a furry gray ball, which wiggles and stretches itself back into the shape of a mole and begins to snuffle its way across the gravel.

Richard puts on his mitten and bends to pick it up. He stands with it in his hand, and it turns its pointed pink nose toward his fuzzy blue thumb. It buzzes in alarm, or perhaps to threaten, and he feels its struggling body vibrate through the leather palm of the mitten like a rapscallion nephew's trick handshake. He steps off the side of the road and puts the mole on the ground. It moves head first into the earth, flat pink gloves swimming it into the mud, and in a few seconds it has disappeared. Richard and Annis watch the surface of the mud break and ripple as the mole tunnels its way below.

"Good rescue," Annis says.

Richard designed the kitchen of the house where he and Eileen live. It's an old farmhouse, but they had the kitchen gutted and rebuilt with high-quality materials and appliances. To plan it Richard spent hours in the empty barn, moving cardboard boxes around a chalked outline on the dirt floor. He would arrange the boxes in one way and roast an imaginary wild goose, plucking and eviscerating it at a cardboard work counter, rinsing it in a cardboard sink, stuffing and trussing it on a platter he remembered from his mother's pantry, and finally bending to place the heavy-bottomed roasting pan laden with oyster-stuffed goose into an oversized gas cardboard oven.

First he placed the false oven at waist height behind an imaginary door in the make-believe wall; then he tried a regulation oven in a traditional stove at standard height. Finally he selected the traditional gas stove, though with an oversized oven that would accommodate two roasting pans, and therefore two wild geese, at once. Along with his talent for gourmet cooking, Richard is a man with great affection for tradition. He will bend at the waist to place his future geese in his oven just as his mother bent to place cookies and chickens and macaroni and cheese in the ovens of his youth.

Richard owns the Bible that was given to his father when he was eight. Richard is an atheist, but now and then he reads a Biblical passage or two: he's an educated man. Whenever he reads the Bible, though, his mind wanders; he can't follow the lesson, he loses track of the narrative of begats. Instead of small print on an ecru page he sees a hot October day under a clear heartbreaking sky, the hot wind wrapping the skirts of the several women around their knees, them pressing the skirts down with purse- and program-stuffed hands. The words that the minister beside the open grave speaks are whipped away in the hot wind, out of the cemetery and onto the highway into the path of a SYSCO delivery truck.

The words were about Richard's own father, dead in that hole in the ground. The minister was a close friend of the dead father; for more than twenty years, any Thursday night might find them in the dead man's study, playing poker. The minister knew Richard's father as well as anyone on God's green earth ever knew him; Richard might have learned a lot about his father that hot October day if he only could have heard the minister's words. The minister was weeping as he spoke, but his tears didn't weigh down the words enough to keep the wind from sweeping them up

over the split rail fence and across the asphalt to
meet their own doom on the chrome grill of a
trailer truck delivering prepared food.

"Richard," Annis says. "Come on out.
We've got a calf on the way."

Richard drives out to Annis and Chip's
ranch, which is eighteen miles upstream and five
hundred feet higher in elevation than his place.
From their living room window they can see the
entire valley spread out like a diorama before them.
Standing outside, waiting for Annis, Richard
imagines he can see tiny Lewises and Clarks in
coonskin caps paddling along the stretch of river
that glistens between miniature fields of alfalfa and
stands of toy ponderosa pines.

They drive a couple of miles farther up the
road and park beside the pasture where the cow
selected for Richard lies. Annis rolls the window
down. A plume of cold mist billows in, and right
behind it the sound of the cow's screams. She
closes the window again. They sit in the truck and
watch the cow through binoculars. Even though
Annis keeps the engine running and has the heater
on full blast, Richard's feet go numb, then begin to
hurt. It rained in the night and the grass is gray with
rainwater, except for the patch of flat bright green
grass where the cow has been straining. Except for
that flat patch, the grass stands straight up, sharp
little sentinels watching the cow suffer.

"We're going to have to pull that calf,"
Annis mutters. She puts the truck in gear, but just
as she starts to pull into the road the calf suddenly
slides right out of the mom's rear end, a black
slithy tove in a mass of silver phlegm.

"Oh!" Richard says. It's such a surprise

and a relief.

Annis smiles at him and puts the truck back in park.

The mom cow licks and licks and licks the calf, and after another very long time – *too long,* Annis mutters, *too long* – the calf starts trying to stand up. Again and again it gets to its knees, raises one end or the other, and topples. The mother cow licks the toppled end and shoves at the reluctant end with her nose, but the calf can't stand up.

A feeling of doom starts easing into Richard's heart, and after a while of watching the mother try too long to lick the calf upright, he doesn't want to watch any more.

"Annis," he says, "I've got to go."

"It's too big," she says. "We'll have to bring it in." She puts the truck in gear again and they drive back to Richard's car.

He gets out and watches her drive on down to the lower field where Chip and the hired man are spreading feed for a crowd of cows with healthy calves in attendance. Then he drives home with numb feet.

Richard practiced law in a small town in northern California for more than thirty years. His practice ran the gamut from divorce to theft, extortion to murder, abandonment to wife abuse to child support and, more than once, to traffic violations. Over the course of those thirty years he raised four children, divorced his first wife, fell in love with three other women, buried his parents and his only brother, and never traveled outside of the United States. He has never even gone to Vancouver, British Columbia. He knows he's a thin, meaningless failure of a man, forever the bantamweight he was in high school, dancing around the ring on knobbly little legs and talking too much. He fell hard for Eileen, who left her then husband for him. They're happy together. He has only money to offer her, though he thinks she doesn't really understand that yet.

He can't stop thinking about Annis.

Richard's father was an attorney for forty-seven years. Retirement was not so fashionable, nor so affordable, in his father's day as it is in his own. Also, his father never got tired of work. His father stayed late at the office, took on many a pro bono case, far more often than he had any moral obligation to do. He was a mild man with the same strawberry hair and speckled skin that Richard has. He had different hobbies, though: he liked hunting for all manner of creatures, birds and deer and bears. He liked swimming. In the summer, when Richard's mother moved to their lake cabin, he would drive up there on Friday night and arrive in the dark. When Richard was small he waited just inside the front door and heard the car turn onto the road a quarter mile away, grind up the rutted road and stop. Richard, his heart beating, heard the car door squeak, and he knew his father was getting out of the car. The door slammed, and Richard could hear his father bend to untie his wingtips. He really could hear his father's belt being unbuckled, the buckle clinking as he stepped out of his trousers. The whisper of a shirt dropping to the ground; then silence as his father walked naked down to the lake, and maybe Richard heard the splash, felt the shock, saw the smooth ripples as his father dove into the cold black water.

Richard could hardly contain himself as he

waited for his father to finish swimming. Looking back, he isn't sure why he was so filled with excitement: every week for three months, every year for fifteen years, his father came out on summer weekends and swam before coming inside for a late supper. Maybe it was hunger: Richard and his brother had to wait for their father before they could eat supper. It was dark, and summertime: it must have been nine o'clock at night. It was hunger that made a boy's heart pound, made the boy shiver and hug himself and shift from foot to foot as he waited beside the closed door of the cottage.

And then his father was dripping on the porch, carrying his clothes and his weekend suitcase as he opened the door and said in his mild voice, "Naked I come among you," just in case there was a visiting sister-in-law, or, in later years, a girlfriend of one of the boys, inside setting the table. Whoever she was, she would have been forewarned and would duck into the kitchen while Richard's naked father, looming bright in the kerosene light, left footprints through the great room and up the stairs. He would reappear in the washed-out pants and loose undershirt that was his costume until he left again before dawn on Monday. He came downstairs in those old clothes and everyone sat down at the table and Richard could have his supper at last.

Annis and Chip lived for a long time in the city and then when they were ready they moved to the valley. Annis used to be a nun and Chip was a priest. The usual story. If they hadn't told him – they manage to work it into the conversation within seven minutes of meeting any new person –

Richard would never have guessed.

He'd said, "So where you from?" and she said not *St. Louis* but *a convent in St. Louis.* It's like saying *I was in prison for seven years* or *I am a Mormon* or *I was morbidly obese until I had my stomach stapled* or *I'm legally blind* or *I eat meat.* No matter what the condition, a certain percentage of potential friends will take themselves out of the running when they discover a certain thing about you. *I smoke* will relieve you of certain friends, while *I smoke dope* will take care of others.

"It's a conscious policy," Annis told him when he'd known her long enough to ask about it. "Tell me, wouldn't you be pissed if you'd known me for a month or a year and then suddenly I popped out with *by the way, my ex-husband is God?*"

Chip tends to joke about it. "In my celibate days," he'll begin, and those who just met him will get ready for a funny story. Those who know him better will look at him respectfully, waiting for the nugget of truth he's about to reveal about himself. Those who've known him for a long time will suppress a yawn and sneak a look at the clock on the wall.

People love Chip, though. Richard loves him. He's a wonderful man in many ways. He loves those cows, even though he plans their deaths before they're even conceived. "The children he never had," Eileen once muttered when they were watching Chip do something to a cow, feed or brand or impregnate. But Richard didn't think that was quite it.

On Sunday the sixteenth of March Richard and Eileen go to the corned beef supper at the

Grange. They stand in line at the window and three women behind the counter heap their plates with corned beef and cabbage and potatoes and plenty of yellowish juice. "Want an onion?" Margaret Aspinall asks Richard, and he says he does.

Eileen carries her food across the room to sit with her friends from the book club and Richard sits down beside Chip, across from Annis. Rona Barta, beside Annis, is telling everyone within earshot and beyond about her new marble counter tops.

"Deep green, marbled with silver and these absolutely gorgeous streaks of ruby red." She might be describing what Richard, sitting across from her, sees when he looks at her, since she talks without first swallowing her bites of corned beef and cabbage. "Glossy. I'm telling you, when the sun comes in there of a morning I can't hardly keep my eyes open. I have to wear my Ray-Bans in my own new kitchen!" She bellows like a calving cow.

It's so loud in the Grange Hall you have to, to let people know you're laughing hard.

The Grange always hypes the home-made nature of their dinners, but it's not the kind of home-made Richard grew up with. Though he suspects they do use the same potato flakes to make their mashed potatoes. But the cake is probably purchased from SYSCO. Light and melts in your mouth, as if it's hardly there. His mother's cakes – now *those* were cakes. Dense and moist and dripping with frosting, you'd eat a few bites and they would settle into some cranny at the bottom of your stomach next to the entrance to the intestine and rest there for hours afterwards. That was *cake*.

Rona's husband Lloyd is the current Grand Poobah of the Grange. Richard can't keep track of these things. There's Grangers and Masons and Elks and the Klan and the Christian Fellowship down at the intersection, and each one has a Grand Poobah. Over time he's learned that even egalitarian groups, like the Wymmin's Coven and the Forest Partnership, though they purport to be all for one and one for all, they have Poobahs too. They bow to the east, bow to the west, they do the hootchy-kootchy and they hope for the best, and God, or a spirit in a fir tree, smiles down on them.

Annis is leaning across the table, telling him something. As he looks at her earnest face the light catches on the thick edges of her spectacles and suddenly he sees her as an alien creature, someone come down from a distant planet to dwell among them for a spell.

"What?" he says.

"After we fetched that calf in the truck I could hear her mom for hours," she says.

He can hear her now, bawling in animal grief as the calf is taken away.

"It didn't ever thrive," Annis says. "It was too big."

I thought his eyes were piercing, but now, close up, I see that they are pale and milky. When he first looks at something he blinks rapidly several times. His eyes are tucked under red-rimmed lids with sparse pink lashes, and the lids themselves are topped off with hoods, little pouches of flesh that hang from the top of his eye sockets. And at the corner of each eye are a thousand wrinkles. And in the wrinkles lies the dust of many years.

Down in town at the Manor Richard's old mom, still alive, hands Richard a newspaper clipping headlined *Pancreatic Cancer Has No Symptoms.*

Dear Dr. Dan, it reads, *My husband has been diagnosed with pancreatic cancer. The doctor says he has two months to live. Why didn't we have any warning?*

"Doesn't this sound just like me?" she says.

He looks at her over the tops of his glasses. "You *have* lost weight in the last year or so."

"I can't eat a thing," she says.

"You always seem to have a good appetite when I take you out somewhere," he says.

"Well, Ricky, think about it. Could it have something to do with the food? The stuff they serve here – *no* one wants to eat it. Great plateloads go back to the kitchen."

"Well," he says. "So what do you want to do about the pancreatic cancer?"

"Nothing," she says. "I'm ready to go."

Eileen is a mystery to Richard. She has no idiosyncracies. No stray hairs straggle over her temples, she has almost never lost her temper in his presence, they've been together for years. He'll be out in the pasture and look down the fenceline and see her trudging along the ditch in her black Wellingtons, head down, staring at the brown dead grass that he sprayed out (against the rules) two weeks ago and seeing – how could he know what she sees? He doesn't know.

She does have passions. Once a year she travels with her sister to shrines, retreats, birthplaces of sacred individual. They've gone to Jerusalem, to Tibet, to Sedona. She describes the rituals they've watched and joined: baptisms, purifications, sweat lodges, exorcisms, healing ceremonies. The photographs she brings back show her and her sister drinking in bars with pilgrims and supplicants and priests.

Richard might have gone with her if she'd asked.

Annis and Chip don't raise cows for a living, they just like having them, much the way some people like throwing pots. They like growing cows for other people to kill later. Really, it's beyond Richard's comprehension.

The year of his dead calf there is also a dwarf one, born all hunch-backed with its four legs too close together, as if it's folded up in the middle. It sort of skips when it walks, a little hunchy black calf skipping through the straw. It doesn't last long. There are also some giant twins that are so big they kill their mother as they get born. And once when Richard goes out to the ranch there's a uterus hanging out the back of a cow, and though it had been funny on the TV show to see James Herriott with his entire arm thrust into a cow's female region, making faces as her muscles heaved and rippled, Richard finds it less hilarious to see a red sac dangling from the rear end of a frightened black cow running heavily across a frosty field.

Disease, too. Always the fear of hoof and mouth. Always the specter of mad cow.

The local feds and some local critics of the federal departments that employ them – among them Lloyd Barta, the current Grand Poobah of the Grange – have spent several years planning and executing The Perfect Cut, and on a spring Saturday they invite the Community to a

Demonstration Pre-Commercial Thin. With a dozen other people, Richard and Annis climb aboard a decommissioned school bus that's been painted green and are driven past the Grange, past Annis and Chip's ranch, up into the mountains to the end of the paved road, then over kidney-rattling gravel for a couple of miles. The bus pulls up in front of a barn, and with much adult laughter the passengers step out.

"God what a day," Lloyd says.

It's clear, and the very air is blue and crisp with thin spring light. Annis and Richard follow Lloyd and the rest of the people across a damp pasture and up a path between stands of pine. Shooting stars, *Dodecatheon meadia*, grow beneath the pines, and here and there they're so thick the wave of sunlit magenta hurts the eyes.

A federal employee points them out. "Among other benefits," she says, "the thinning has resulted in increased sunlight on the forest floor, which has produced a bumper crop of shooting stars."

But Richard can't be bothered to comment today. The consistency of the air, the shouting of the jays and warblers in the trees, the magenta carpet and even the motley clutch of people traipsing through the woods; *everything* strikes him as miraculous this morning. Walking through the woods on a spring day with a friend and a crowd of strangers, hoping that someone has found a way to save the world! *Everyone* hoping that! What more could you want? The buzz of a Pacific mole in the palm. A free-range chicken roasting in high heat. Twelve princesses emerging at midnight from under the ground to dance with twelve princes till dawn. The promise of that *every* night! The hope every year for a soft cool spring!

"Chee-rist," Lloyd Barta says, falling back to walk on Annis's left side. "Day like this makes anyone believe in God."

Shock and awe. The perfect cut.

HAPPY HOUR

Late in the day we go out to the Home for Happy Hour. It's a little custom we have when I'm on the Cape now; I buy a nice bottle of Chardonnay, or one of Beaujolais, and round about four o'clock I pack my aged mother into my rented car and we drive to the edge of town, where the handsome, gleaming Home houses the ancient and the crippled.

I drop my mother off at the front door and watch her totter in, carrying her cane. When I'm not here she comes on the old folks' bus, and pokes along through the halls, nodding and smiling and stopping to say hello to any oldsters parked along the wall. At this time of day, though, most of the inhabitants are already enured in their rooms, propped up in chairs watching Oprah, so my mother makes her way with expedition down to the end of the South East Corridor to the room where Me Old Dad lives.

I park in *VISITORS* and follow in my mother's footsteps, lugging the liter of today's flavor through the bright lobby and past the reproductions of fine art on the walls. I'm fond of the Home, which has a good reputation; I like to think it was a coup to get my father into it. The corridors smell of beef and lemon cleanser, and the nursing station at the top of

Dad's section is empty except for Violet Kennedy, who reclines beside it in a padded chair, taking her sweater off.

"Hello, Mrs. Kennedy," I say, and Violet looks at the ceiling and cries "Help me!" in the ugliest old voice you can imagine, but it doesn't bother me any more.

In every room an old slumpy person is staring at a TV. "Get your hair out of your eyes, Martha," I hear a crone from 211 shout. "You'd be prettier if you'd use a comb."

Halfway down the hall Bobbi is standing at the mobile Meds Cart, mixing drugs in a cup. "I'm on my way down," she says brightly.

Aren't we all? I think, but out loud I say, "See you there."

As I arrive at Dad's little pink room Martin the tall Jamaican man and Ella the very pretty young woman from Brazil are lifting my father out of his bed.

"Okay, turn now," Martin says, "turn, turn, turn to me."

I could listen to his musical voice forever.

Dad's old feet patter on the linoleum floor as he tries to help Martin and Ella turn him, and then Martin says, "Okay, now, Mr. Williams, here is the chair behind your bum," and they lower Dad into the wheelchair. Martin moves in behind him and grasps him under the arms, and Ella leans over in front, and they shift him to the left, and Ella stuffs a cushion between his hip and the side of the chair.

"Okay now, Mr. Williams?" Martin says, bending over to be at Dad's eye level, and I can see Dad's head slightly, slightly nod. "See you later then," Martin says, and Ella caresses his shoulder and says, "See you later, Mr. Williams," and they smile at my mother and come out of the room, and smile at me and say "Hello" as they pass.

My mother is pulling dead leaves off the foil-wrapped plants on the windowsill, left over from the most recent Happy Holiday.

"Hi, Dad," I shout from the door, and I walk past the bed where Harry died, to Dad's side of the room.

Dad slowly, slowly, slowly turns his head toward me, and his hand lifts slightly from the arm of his chair.

"Bill, can't you say hello?" my mother says.

The faintest of whispers issues from Dad.

"Hi, Dad," I say again.

"*I'll* say it then," my mother says. *"Hello, Vera."*

"He *did* say hello," I say. How on earth do they manage when I'm not here? "Mom, do you have your hearing aids in?"

"What?" she says. She looks at Dad. "Did you say hello?"

He slowly, slowly turns his face toward her. He slightly, slightly nods.

"Oh, damn," she says. "This damn thing." She cups her hand beside her right ear, then her left ear, and shakes her head. "The battery's dead again."

The batteries in my mother's hearing aids seem to die at the drop of a hat. "Do you have any with you?" I shout.

"What?" she shouts back.

"Batteries," I call.

"I *have* batteries," she says.

"Want me to – " I hold out my hand.

"What do *you* want them for?" she says.

"I'll Put Them In For You," I say, enunciating clearly and pointing to her purse, to her hearing aid, to my own chest.

She shakes her head. "I can do it," she says, and she sits down in the Visitor's Chair and takes the hearing aid out of her left ear and begins rooting through her purse in search of her spare battery case.

"How you doing, Dad?" I say.

"What?" my mother says, looking up.

"I'M ASKING DAD HOW HE IS," I shout.

"I can't *hear* you," she says, waving her hearing aid. "Wait till I put the new battery in."

I look at Dad. "How you doing, Dad?" I whisper.

"As well as can be expected," is what I'm sure he whispers back.

"Care for a drink?"

"Yes," he says very clearly.

I pull the bottle of Beaujolais out of its brown paper wrapper and, holding it against my forearm, present it to Me Old Dad as if I were wearing a tux and he were a young buck of seventy sitting close to a buxom blonde at a white-linen-covered table for two. He nods very, very slightly. With a flourish I pull a corkscrew from the pocket of my denim jacket and proceed to open the bottle of wine.

"There." My mother taps at her ear. The battery is installed and the hearing aid replaced, and she can hear again. Pretty well. "What is it?" she says.

"Beaujolais," I say.

"Oh, Daddy's favorite," she says. She leans forward and pats his knee. "Isn't it, Bill?"

He slowly turns his face toward her and slightly nods.

I take three plastic cups out of my father's handkerchief drawer, set them on the adjustable

table, and fill each of them half full of dark wine. My mother takes a straw from the cache in his sock drawer, unwraps it and sticks it into one of the cups, and, holding the cup up to his face, inserts the end of the straw between his lips.

I take a drink of my Beaujolais.

My father sucks, but his straw remains empty. My mother pulls it out of his mouth and reinserts it. My father sucks again, and the straw turns pink, and Beaujolais is delivered to the target. My mother removes the straw from his mouth and sets down the cup and picks up her own and takes a healthy swig.

"Mmm," she says. She holds it up toward me. "Good!" She looks at Dad. "You like?"

He lifts his eyes toward her and slightly, slightly nods.

With a rattle and a whir, Bobbi and the Meds Cart appear outside the door. "Ah, Happy Hour," Bobbi says. She bustles around the cart, opening containers and pouring sludge into a cup, and she rustles across the room, stirring as she comes, and gets right up close to Dad and says, "Here's your Sinemet and your Requip and your potassium supplement and your Paxil, Mr. Williams."

Dad opens his mouth and she spoons in the medicated pulp.

"What's it in?" I say, and Bobbi says, "A little chocolate ice cream, with thickener to make it go down easily."

"Must taste good with wine," I say.

"Oh, Vera!" My mother laughs as if I am the wittiest comic on the face of God's green earth. I wonder what she thinks I said.

Bobbi puts her hand on Dad's shoulder and leans close to gaze into his eyes. "Did it all go down?" she says, and he slightly nods. She pats him and steps back. "Want some orange juice to wash it down?"

"No," he says clearly, and he motions with his left hand, the stronger one, toward the table in front of him.

"He wants more wine," my mother says, and she picks it up.

"I'll have someone bring some in anyway," Bobbi says briskly.

It is nearly five o'clock on a February evening and the world outside my father's windows is going dark. Evening is my second favorite time of day in the Home, after early morning, when things have not yet begun to hop. In the evening the inmates are tucked into their own rooms and the people who mop and clean and instigate therapy have gone home for the day. The only people around now are the ones who medicate, the ones who lift and turn and carry and prop, the ones who feed. Except for two dozen televisions and Mrs. Kennedy calling for help, it is quiet. It's especially pleasant since Dad's last roommate has not yet been replaced.

("How's Harry?" I asked during a phone call last month.

"Dead," said Dad. He didn't seem much bothered. He expects to die himself one of these days.)

My father's windows look down on the back door, where trucks deliver things and hearses pick up corpses. Beyond that driveway is a playground where the children of the Home's employees cavort in fine weather, jerky little urchins in bright colors who yell and toddle and swing and weep. On the hillside beyond them is a grove of scrawny oaks whose leaves have turned from green to gold to brown to gone in the months Dad has lived in his little pink room. Two red-tailed hawks sometimes sail down the sky above the oaks, together or alone, at leisure or pursued by crows. The flittering drops of brightest yellow you see from time to time are American goldfinches.

My mother, never one to sit still when she can putter, is now taking Dad's clean clothes from a clear plastic bag and putting them into his five drawers. "Someone mixed the white with the colored," she says, holding up a pair of pink socks.

"I don't care," Dad says.

She looks up. "What?" She looks at me.

"He doesn't care," I say loudly.

"Of course not," she says, bending again to her labor. "He never cared what he looked like."

"Ready for more wine?" I say to Dad, and I think he nods, so I lift his cup and insert the straw between his lips. He sucks mightily and nothing happens.

"You have to put it in farther." My mother has abandoned her putting-away of clothes in order to monitor my work.

I pull out the straw, my father's lips open another smidgeon, and I plunge the straw deep into the interior, sure it is shredding the soft red tissues of his cheeks. He sucks, and the straw darkens. After a moment I say, "Get enough?" and he slightly nods, and I pull away the straw.

The clean laundry stowed, my mother sits again in the Visitor's Chair. She leans toward my father. "Did you get enough?"

"Yes," he says clearly.

"Orange juice?" It is Millicent, another of the beautiful Brazilian women who take care of my father and his fellow incarcerees.

"Oh, yes," my mother says. "Bill, look, Millicent has brought your orange juice."

"Thank you," Dad says to Millicent, who has crossed the room and placed the cup of bright liquid on the table beside the empty wine cups and the half-full bottle.

"You're welcome, Mr. Williams," she says. She smooths his hair briefly with the palm of her hand, as if conferring blessedness.

"Bill, say thank you," my mother says. She looks up at Millicent. "Thank you, Millicent."

"You're welcome, Mrs. Williams," she says. She smiles at my mother, and she smiles at me as she walks by.

I smile very hard back at her. I try always to look like a great obsequious pool of middle-aged gratitude to these young people from foreign lands who take care of my father and smile at my mother. I would like to give them money, but they can't accept it. I would like to give them gifts, but I don't. I would like to tell them all how much I appreciate their kindness and their willingness to do this work, but if I try to say more to them than a few words of greeting I start to sob and can only blurt clogged unintelligible monosyllables.

"She is so cute," my mother says. "Isn't she, Bill?"

He turns his eyes toward her and nods slightly.

"Well, *I* think she's very cute," my mother says. "Do you know, she has a thirteen-year-old daughter?"

"She does?" I say. Millicent looks about twenty-two years old.

"That's Emilia," Dad whispers.

"Yes, she does," my mother says. "She and

her husband both work here."

"Emilia?" I say.

"No, Millicent," my mother says.

"Emilia has the daughter," my father says.

"Dad says it's Emilia who has the daughter," I say.

My mother shakes her head. "Bill, that was *Millicent*." She reaches over and tucks the towel more securely around his neck.

My father clears his throat. "Emilia has the thirteen-year-old daughter," he says.

"What?" My mother leans close to him, placing her ear directly in front of his mouth.

My father gathers his energy and says loudly, "Emilia has the thirteen-year-old daughter."

My mother shakes her head and sits back. She looks at me. "I can't hear him, can you?"

"DAD SAYS IT'S EMILIA WHO HAS THE THIRTEEN-YEAR-OLD DAUGHTER," I shout.

She looks at him in surprise. "Are you sure? I was sure that was Millicent."

"It was *Millicent* who brought the juice, but *Emilia* has the daughter," I say loudly.

"Well," my mother says. "Bill, are you going to drink that or not?"

Dad nods, and my mother removes the straw from his wine cup and puts it into his o.j. and holds it to his mouth, and bit by bit, without pause and with great effort, he drinks it all in.

"Shall we have another?" My mother is holding up her plastic cup, and, never one to refuse wine, I pour one for her and one for me.

She picks up a hand cloth from the night stand and wipes pink spittle from my father's beard.

"More for you, Dad?" I say.

"No," he says.

"Well," my mother says. "Here we are."

"Okay, quiz time," I say. "Who is Dr. McDonough's favorite poet?"

Yesterday my father and I rode the cripples' bus to his neurologist's office. After only a twenty-minute wait the nurse beckoned, and I pushed Me Old Dad into the inner sanctum, where Dr. McDonough shook his hand, said he hoped they're treating him well at the Home, and asked if he'd written any poetry lately.

"No," my father said. "I can't write."

Dr. McDonough looked at me.

"He can't write any more," I said.

"That would be a problem," Dr. McDonough said. He sat down and crossed his legs at the ankle. "My son writes poetry. None published yet, though. I have never written, but I love the poetry of Gerard Manley Hopkins." He looked at my father. "You know Hopkins?" he said in a louder voice.

"Nothing is so beautiful as spring," my father said.

Dr. McDonough remained as expressionless as a man lacking dopamine. "Yes," he said in a noncommittal fashion.

"It's why we're here," I said. "That he can't write. We were hoping there's some last little thing you can do, some drug, to squeeze a bit more function from the limbs."

"Ah, yes," said Dr. McDonough. "When the brain cells are dead, there's little bringing them back."

"Glory be to God for dappled things, for skies of couple-colour as a brinded cow," my father said.

"What's that?" said Dr. McDonough.

Now I say it again. "Dr. McDonough's favorite poet."

"Oh, that three-named man," my mother says, for I had summarized the visit for her yesterday, once Dad, exhausted, had reported back to quarters and been put to bed. "Gerald Something Hopkins."

"Two points for Mother," I say. "Okay. Here's the next one. Has Dr. McDonough's son been published yet?"

"His son?" my mother says.

"No," my father says.

"Got it," I say, pointing my rapidly-emptying cup at my father. "Here's the clincher. What is the physical condition of Dr. McDonough's seventeen-year-old daughter?"

"I didn't know he had a daughter," my mother says.

"Virgin," says Dad.

"You win!" I cry.

"A *virgin?*" my mother says, having heard my father's last word distinctly.

My father's face seems to indicate amusement, and I believe he is vibrating slightly with laughter.

"As Dr. McDonough sat reading the paper one night, he overheard his daughter and her friend in the kitchen, discussing their love lives," I explain to my mother. "His daughter said, *I'm still a virgin.* It made Dr. McDonough's heart swell with joy." Dr. McDonough had paused yesterday, pen poised to up Dad's Requip another half-mil, to tell us this. "Okay, Final Question, fifty points. What is Dr. McDonough's daughter's friend's opinion of Dr. McDonough's daughter's lack of sexual experience?"

My mother is busily draining her plastic cup of dregs.

"Not missing much," my father says, and his mouth breaks into the shape of a grin and his eyes squeeze closed. He is laughing indeed.

"One more for the road," my mother says, and she fills her cup and mine, and even though I am now the designated driver for life, I do not stop her.

How did this happen? How can I be so pleased to see my father tucked in here in this sparkling, barrier-free circumscribed existence? I know the answer to that one: after the years of quarreling about the sharp-edged end tables, treacherous footstools, slippery throw rugs and precarious lamps in my parents' house; after the months of forcing visiting nurses and home health aides and grab-bar installers through their front door; after the Days of No-More-Driving Rage, when the summer air was so heavy with furious shouting about the *car* that I might be forgiven for thinking I'd fallen through the looking glass back into my adolescence; after these long years of decline and fall and fall, how can I be anything but pleased to have Dad safely in the Home?

And surely they are too. For every time they gave in, relinquished another acre of territory, accepted another piece of undesired help, we sighed and sat down for Happy Hour, and (as long as Dad could talk and hold his glass) they'd lift their drinks and marvel *What would we do without you!*

The Home. It is, perhaps, what I think he thought he always wanted: a total life of the mind, nothing to do but think and read. Well, of course he loved to eat, too, and he has said that he sometimes longs for *crackers and peanut butter* or *a celery stalk filled with cream cheese* or *apple pie unpuréed.*

My mother, too, despite her mild stroke, has everything she'd wanted: the house is hers again, she can entertain her friends (too late for that, of course, since all her friends are dead except Mrs. Rager, who is mad, and Margie Caviglia, who lies bedridden in her own home, attended by an angry daughter). She shops, she reads, she sleeps as late as she wants to, and she takes the Council on Aging bus to the Home four days a week to feed my father his puréed lunch. Then she takes the same bus home again, brings in the mail, and sits down in the blue chair to read *Martha Stewart Living.*

"I keep thinking I'm going to stop taking that," she has said more than once, "but then I think, *just one more year.*"

There's a bumping at the door, and the sound of labored breathing. My father moves his eyes in that direction and then turns his head the other way and says, as if thoroughly sickened, "Oh, *god.*"

My mother has heard nothing.

I turn around and see an old fart struggling to disengage the wheel of his chair from the edge of the door. He is panting with the effort, working hard, whether to move forward or to back up I can't tell.

"Goodness," I say to my father. "Who's that?"

"It's Mr. Henderson."

He says it in such a tone of disgust that I laugh, and suddenly my father laughs, too.

"Does he come often?" I say.

"Yes," my father says, his eyes closed.

"What?" says my mother suspiciously. "What are you laughing at?"

"At Mr. Henderson," I say, leaning toward

her and motioning with my head toward the door.

She looks quickly. "Oh, *that* man again!" she says. "Vera, push the button, push the button." She waves her hand toward the call button clipped to Dad's blanket.

"Push the button?" I say.

"Yes, *push the button*," she says. "Someone will come and get him."

Mr. Henderson groans. I reach over and push the button. "What's wrong with him?"

"He goes through Daddy's drawers," my mother says.

"He comes in and sits looking at me," Dad says.

"God forbid," I say. We watch Mr. Henderson trying to move, pushing and then pulling at the wheel of his chair. He grunts with the effort. I should do something – go give him a hand, alert a nurse. "Is the light on?" I lean over to peer at the light beside my father's bed.

"Yes, it's on," my mother says. "They can see it in the hall. You have to wait."

"Sometimes it takes half an hour for them to answer," my father says.

"*What* are you saying, Bill?" my mother says.

"He says sometimes it takes half an hour for them to answer," I say loudly. "That's terrible. What if you need to go to the bathroom?"

"I wait," my father says. "They have other people to take care of."

"He has an accident," my mother says.

"I'm never one of the others," Dad says.

Mr. Henderson has managed to back out of the doorway, and I catch a glimpse of the back of his chair as he starts rolling himself up the hall.

"You're what, Bill?" my mother says, leaning toward him.

"Never one of the others."

"Never one of the others!" She frowns at him. "*What* are you talking about?"

If Lucifer himself sat down to design a hell for Me Old Dad, this would surely be it: my father, descendant of Irish talkers, long a long story teller himself, a long-winded lecturer, a writer and reciter of poetry, a declaimer of the Chaucerian English he learned to *rede and speke* thanks to the GI Bill, an actor and director of Shakespeare's plays and a lover of the sonnets, a man who often sang in a lovely tenor that he came to the garden alone, can barely speak above a whisper, clearly, or for long. For the last two years he and my mother lived together they were the Jack & Mrs. Sprat of miscommunication: he couldn't speak, she couldn't hear.

For her, the inability to hear him may have been a bit of heaven on earth after fifty-odd – *very* odd – years of listening to him go on.

The smell of beef – really, the *aroma* of beef – has made its way into my father's little pink room. The supper hour approaches. I have eaten food here and it is quite good; the meat is tender, the coffee is hot, and the vegetables are often surprisingly close to *al dente*. Of course, that last – *al dentism* – is something my father can no longer appreciate. Nor, really, is tenderness an issue in meat that is puréed. And by the time the cup is lifted, the straw properly inserted, and sufficient vacuum pressure applied to draw liquid into his mouth, his coffee has had a chance to cool. But for his first few months here, before his ability to lift food to his mouth and swallow it had declined to its present sorry state, Dad was able to enjoy the Home's carefully prepared meals: a bit of crunch in his chicken salad, a crispy crust of breadcrumbs on his Friday filet of sole, buttered toast that was (astonishingly!) still hot when his breakfast tray arrived.

Along with the fragrance of beef comes Martin. "I see your light is on, Mr. Williams," he says. "Is there something you need?"

"No," my father says. "It was Mr. Henderson."

"It was that man who comes in here," my mother says.

Martin smiles. "I saw Mr. Henderson coming away from this room," he said. "I thought, Maybe that is why Mr. Williams has his light on!"

We all laugh in delight. Happy Hour is nearing its close.

"Supper is on the way, Mr. Williams," Martin says. "I will be helping you tonight, you and Mrs. Salamone and Mrs. Wolf across the hall."

"Oh, good," my mother says. "He'll like that. Won't you, Bill?" She leans forward. "You like Martin to feed you, don't you?"

"I like *you* to feed me," my father says.

She frowns and turns her ear toward his mouth. "What?"

"I like you to feed me," he says again.

She shakes her head and looks at me.

"He likes *you* to feed him," I say.

She sits back. "Bill, I have to take *Vera* home and feed *her*," she says. She looks at Martin. "I have to take my baby home and feed *her* supper!"

"Ah," Martin says. "This is your baby?" He smiles at me.

"My little baby," my mother says.

I glance at my father; he is staring expressionlessly at me. "I know, I know," I whisper. "You'd hate to be hanging by your thumbs since I was a baby." His lips move; he is sticking out his tongue at me. I stick mine out at him.

"I too am my mother's baby," Martin says. "She will always think so."

We smile at each other, big baby, old baby. He can't be more than twenty-five. As I smile I hear a *craaack* as the thin lines that have begun to erode the edges of my lips gain another millimeter.

"I will be back in a little bit," Martin says.

"Time to head out, Mom?" I say.

"I guess so," she says. She is blotting saliva from the sleeve of my father's shirt.

I put the cork back in the neck of the Beaujolais bottle. There's not much left, but I lift it and say jovially, "*This* goes home with *us*!"

"Bill, how's your wine supply?" my mother says.

"Fine," he says. "FINE."

It's written on his chart: *6 ounces of wine with evening meal.* Every couple of weeks someone rolls my father downstairs to the business office, where he withdraws nine dollars from his Personal Expenses account, and someone – Jennifer, Kathy, my mother – replenishes his wine supply.

It's not a bad life: beautiful women to bathe and dress and toilet you, a man with a musical voice to feed you your purée, six ounces of cheap white wine with every evening meal.

Is it?

The evening meal arrives, borne into the room by Heather from Dietary. "Hul-lo, Mr. Williams," she says, waiting for my mother to whisk away the little plastic cups before she places the tray on his table.

"Hello, Heather," my father says.

"*Hello, Heather*," my mother says. "*Thank you, Heather.*"

"You're welcome, Mrs. Williams," Heather says. She lifts the covers off the dishes and carries them out the door.

"Let's see what you've got," my mother says, leaning over the tray. On the dinner plate are three lovely scoops of supper, one brown, one white, one orange. On another plate is a little golden ball of dessert.

"Did someone make that or do it?" I ask.

"Did it," my father says.

"They do it down in the kitchen," my mother says. She's peering at the weekly menu taped to my father's door. "*Rib-eye steak, potatoes, carrots. Apple pie.* Do you want me to get you started?"

"I'll go get the car," I say. "Mom, I'll meet you out front."

"All right, dear." She's loading a spoon with a bolus of mashed potatoes. "I'll just get Daddy started. If Martin has to feed three of them it will take him a while to get here."

"I'm never one of the others," Dad says.

"Goodnight, Dad," I say, and kiss the top of his old white head. "See you tomorrow."

But his attention is focused on the mashed potatoes now zeroing in on his mouth.

"Mom, I'm going," I say.

"All right, dear," she says, not looking away from her work. "Chew, Bill. *Chew.* Now *swallow.*"

Heather and the supper cart are disappearing around the distant corner as I start back up the hall. I nearly collide with Martin as he emerges from Mrs.

Salamone's and Mrs. Wolf's room. We laugh.

"Goodnight," I say.

"Goodnight," he says, and he enters my father's room.

In each room that I pass an old person (or two) sits (mostly) upright, a tray on a table before (usually) her, gazing at the bright colors jittering on the screen at the end of the bed. "Help me," Mrs. Kennedy calls, from her own room now, and I hear someone say, "What do you need, Violet? Here is your apple pie."

Night has fallen. The automatic doors close with a firm *whump* behind me and I walk down the sidewalk past the brightly-lit windows in the rehab wing. Even though these inhabitants will not be here forever, they have no more modesty than the lifers; in nighties or johnnies, they are perched in beds or on chairs in front of trays, watching Emeril cook gumbo, unconcerned that their curtains are open. Perhaps they assume that no one would bother to look in.

The parking lot is nearly empty; not many people visit the Home in the dark. I unlock my car and then walk past it to stand at the edge of the asphalt, staring at the obscurity under the trees. For fifty years I have been coming to the Cape and going away again. My father came and went before me, but is here for the duration now. His father did the same, and lies among others in the ground a few miles away.

What would they do without me? A blade of wind slips out of the woods and scrapes my cheeks, and suddenly, as if my breath had touched a frosted pane of glass, I see clearly that whatever it is, they *are* doing it without me. They have their own lives to live. I'm on my own.

I love the beach, the dunes, the ceaseless roar

of the wine-dark sea, but this is the Cape to me: steep breeze in the oaks, staggering pitch pines, the rank essence of last year's leaves. Faint fragrance of skunk, and a rustling in the underbrush as it pokes its sharp nose into the hummocks of spongy humus that leaves and sand have slowly, slowly manufactured together. A thin moon. Crisp, impassive stars.

There is something very like happiness here in the dark.

"Vera?" My mother is standing at the end of the sidewalk, shading her eyes as she peers across the bright nearly-empty parking lot. "Vera?"

"Coming, Mother," I shout, and I start back to the car. "COMING, MOM."

Has she heard me? For all I know, she thinks I'm the wind.

31933473R00136

Made in the USA
Lexington, KY
01 May 2014